The GREAT ESCAPE

NATALIE HAYNES

SIMON AND SCHUSTER

First published in Great Britain in 2007 by Simon & Schuster UK Ltd
A CBS COMPANY

www.nataliehaynes.com/thegreatescape

1 3 5 7 9 10 8 6 4 2

Simon & Schuster UK Ltd
Africa House
64–78 Kingsway
London WC2B 6AH

www.simonsays.co.uk

A CIP catalogue record for this book
is available from the British Library

ISBN: 978-1-41692-605-4

Typeset in Garamond by M Rules
Printed and bound in Great Britain by
Cox & Wyman Ltd, Reading, Berks

Acknowledgements

I'd like to thank Kate Shaw, Lesley Thorne, and Venetia Gosling for all their sterling work on this book, and equally for their efforts to ensure a future generation of readers.

I should also thank my dad, for his cheery encouragement, and my mum, for being the first to hang out with Millie and Max, and for getting them so completely. I am beyond grateful to Christian Hill for designing and running the website. This book wouldn't have been finished without Dan Mersh, to whom I owe, oh, I don't know, most things.

The Great Escape is dedicated to my grandmother, Georgette. I wish I'd finished it in time for you to read it.

Chapter One

Millie looked at her watch for several seconds before she remembered it was broken. It still glinted sadly at her, water misting its face, with the time stuck immobile at five past ten this morning. She glared at it – it was *supposed* to be waterproof. A bubble popped apologetically by the minute hand, and she sighed heavily. Bad enough to be bored and wet. Worse not to even know how long you'd been there, or how long you had to stay. And she reeked of washing-up liquid, or whatever the stuff was in the bucket. Whichever way you looked at it, her summer holidays were not going well.

Her dad was around the side of the huge, ugly glass box they were cleaning. He was up on the third storey, standing with his friend Bill on the platform, a cradle on ropes which took them up to the higher floors. She could just about hear them laughing, as she scowled at her reflection in the office doors. The security man, sitting at the reception desk, looked back at her in mock alarm. As though she were scowling at *him.* Adults could be so self-centred, she thought, ignoring him. How come Bill and her dad got to have fun together on the platform, while she had to sit down here on her own? No wonder she was bored. But her dad wouldn't let her go up above ground floor, in case she fell.

'It isn't designed for someone as small as you,' he'd explained.

'I'm not small,' she had snapped.

'I know, you're twelve. And for twelve, you're a colossus,' he said.

'Did you just call me fat?'

'Nooooo!' Her dad couldn't help laughing. That was really why she didn't make too much of a fuss. He didn't laugh very much these days. Not since he'd lost his job, anyway.

'What did you call her?' Bill had shouted, loading up their equipment.

'A colossus,' replied Millie. Her dad looked expectant. She rolled her eyes and continued, 'It's a big statue. There was one of the Emperor Nero outside the Colosseum in Rome, that's where it got its name.'

'You've got a pretty smart kid, Alan.'

'Nah,' said Millie, squirming. 'I just have a really dull father.'

'Come here, you!' Her dad had made to chase her, and she'd laughed and dodged out of reach.

*

That had been weeks ago, or at least it felt that way. It was probably just a few hours. Her dad had said she didn't have to come every day, if she didn't want to. She could stay at home, if she preferred, and the woman next door could look in on her from time to time. Millie had given it a nanosecond's thought, weighing up the pros of being able to sit and read in the garden all day against the cons of Mrs Ellis coming round every twenty minutes to ask her what book she was reading, how long it was, what it was about, whether it was as good as Enid Blyton, and so on and so on, until Millie felt like jamming a fork into her own arm, or even Mrs Ellis's arm, either of which would probably be considered rude. She had decided to take the bucket, at least for now, but as choices went, she couldn't help but think it was a lot like being asked if you'd rather be poked in the eye with a sharp pencil or a blunt one.

She had wondered a few times over the past week – since their last visit to clean the windows, in fact – if she'd made the right decision. Last Tuesday, she had been milling around the van, fetching water and adding to it the industrial cleaning fluid that gave her a perpetual scent of washing-up liquid and swimming pools – a perfume people rarely tried to buy from shops – when an estate car had suddenly drawn up outside the back of the office. Millie couldn't work out where on earth it had come from – the building was at the end of a long drive, set back about half a mile from the main road. And that drive stopped at the front of the building. This car seemed to have appeared, fully formed, from the fields behind her, like a metallic shrub. A man had sprung out at her.

'Hello,' he said. 'You're a bit young to be a window cleaner, aren't you?'

'I'm just here helping my . . .' Millie began, before she lost the will and trailed off. If he was going to come up with the same tired joke that every person in every office had come up with so far this summer, she wasn't going to the trouble of giving him a full sentence in return. She wondered if painful predictability and a need to state the obvious came with an office job. Maybe *that* was why her dad had started cleaning windows – to get away from the people in offices. Maybe, she thought, when she left school, she'd become a dentist. They didn't have to deal with people who were too chatty. Still, though, they *did* have to deal with other people's teeth. Urgh. Better than a dentist, she'd become an undertaker – more scope for mistakes, and probably fewer teeth.

'Ah yes. Well, I hope I didn't scare you, coming in the back way.' He must have seen her jump when she heard the engine. 'It's just difficult to get in at the front, you know, with the protesters . . .' He trailed off.

'What protesters?' Millie asked.

'Haven't you . . .? Ah, no, of course, you probably get here too early. They're not up with the larks, are they?'

'I don't know,' Millie replied. She had no idea what time

larks got up. Or what time protesters did. This man was pulling off the rare trick of being both boring *and* a bit weird.

'Well, they're not. But they don't like what we do, so they're here most days, making their point. Well, not *here*, precisely.' The man looked around, as if to reassure himself that a small protest hadn't sprung up behind him, armed with placards, banners, and the occasional klaxon, booing him.

'They're not allowed on our property, obviously – that's trespass. But, you know, they're out on the main road most days, shouting and chanting. It's like a religious cult, if you ask me.'

Millie forbore to point out that she hadn't asked him. But since he was so talkative, she asked the question that had popped into her head the first time he'd mentioned protesters.

'What is it you do that they don't like?'

'Well, you know . . . some people are against any sort of progress at all, and – my goodness I'm running late,' the man said, rushing round to the back of the car as though his shoes were on fire and he kept an extinguisher in the boot for just such an eventuality. 'Must dash. Don't let me keep you.'

Millie assumed he hadn't noticed that she had continued mixing detergent as they spoke, so he really hadn't kept her from anything. He opened the tailgate of the car, and pulled out a trolley, which he stood next to him. He lifted out one crate, then another, placed them on the trolley, then slammed the boot shut. He spun round and pushed his crates quickly towards a small door.

Millie couldn't be quite sure, but she was almost certain she heard meowing.

Chapter Two

'Dad?'

'Yes, love?'

'What do they do there?'

'Where?' Her dad looked bemused. Millie often began conversations as though the other person had been listening to the inside of her head for several moments before she started to speak. Sometimes her dad caught on straight away. Other times, like now, he was a bit slow.

'The Haverham lab.'

'Oh. Scientific research,' he said airily.

'I know it's scientific research, Dad. It's a laboratory. I mean, what *kind* of research?'

'I don't really know. Medical?' He looked too shifty to be telling her the whole truth.

'They're animal testers, aren't they?' Millie said, glaring at him.

'What gave you that idea?' Her dad was playing for time.

'A man told me earlier that there were protesters at the front gate. He had to come in through a back way.'

'Well, people protest against lots of things, love. War, globalisation—'

'Animaltesting.'

'Yes, people do protest against that. But that doesn't mean that's what they do there. It could be anything.' He had now adopted an air of quiet reasonableness that made Millie grind her teeth.

'You think they're conducting a *war* from Haverham?' she asked, her eyebrows raised.

'No.'

'Because that would be a pretty small war, Dad. Will it engulf all of East Anglia, or just Haverham, do you think?'

'OK, they're not protesting about a war. But that doesn't mean it's animal research.'

'The man was delivering crates of cats, Dad.'

'Did you see them?' he asked quickly.

'No. I heard them.' She wasn't going to let this go.

'Well, maybe you misheard.'

'Yes, Dad. Maybe they had a crate of things that meow but weren't cats being taken into a laboratory that has people protesting nearby about how they test on animals.'

'Ah, well . . . still . . .' Her dad seemed to have realised that he was fighting a losing battle.

'No, Dad, still nothing. The cats aren't part of a war effort, are they?'

'I wouldn't think so. Unless the war is on mice.'

'Don't joke, it's not funny.' Millie was resolutely stony-faced.

'I know, Millie, I know. You love cats. They use them for work. It's not funny.'

'It isn't. What if they stick pins in them, like in those pictures?' Millie and her dad had walked past a People for the Ethical Treatment of Animals stand at Strawberry Fair last summer. The pictures they had exhibited had put her off eating meat for life. Ever since, she'd made her dad buy soap and stuff that said it wasn't tested on anything.

'Millie, I know.' He sounded tired. 'I know it's wrong. I don't know exactly what they do, and I don't want to, because I have to work if we're going to eat. Whatever they do won't be any nicer if someone else gets the cleaning work.'

'But Dad, you've seen in through the windows. Have you seen any animals being hurt?'

'No, Millie, I haven't. I promise.' He looked at her and tried to smile, but couldn't quite get it to work in the face of her hard stare. 'I know it's not very nice, but beggars can't be choosers.'

'We're not beggars,' she said softly.

'No, but we will be if I don't clean some windows every day, and their windows once a week. Besides, Bill has a contract with them, and I don't want to let him down. He's been a good friend to us. It's not for ever, love. Just for a while.'

Millie sighed as her dad walked off upstairs.

'You don't need to clean anything. You just need to get another computer job, and we'll be fine.' But she whispered this to herself, because there was no point having this argument again. Her dad had lost his job a few months ago, and had flatly refused to apply for another. Instead, he had spent two weeks sitting in their house, reading constantly and barely going out. Bill had eventually offered him some temporary work in his window-cleaning business, and he had reluctantly accepted. Millie couldn't see why he was being so difficult about things, but Bill told her, rather gruffly, that her dad needed to 'rebuild his confidence'. Millie couldn't see how much more confident her dad needed to be about writing software and virus protection – he'd been doing it her whole life. Longer, in fact – he'd been a computer buff, as he liked to call himself, before she was even born. But at the moment, he seemed incapable of doing anything very much, and she didn't understand why. Nor, she suspected, did Bill, but at least he was trying to help. He had also, she was sure, tried to persuade her dad to go on a date with a desperately boring woman they'd met at Bill's house. Millie's mum had died when she was small, so long ago that she could barely remember her at all, and she did realise her dad needed to spend some time with people who weren't her. But she had been hoping, if not for a fairy godmother, then at least for someone who could talk with authority about something other than her own shoes.

But, ten days later, here she was, back at Haverham. At first, she had been absolutely determined never to come here again. Then she thought that maybe, if she came back, she could find some evidence about what was really going on here. And, if her dad saw that, then he might be persuaded to go and clean somewhere else's windows instead. And then she could write to their MP, which is what her dad had said to do last year, when she was upset by the PETA stand and their pictures. Millie had written, and had received a letter back, saying that her concerns had been noted and would be looked into. Nothing more had come of it.

So here she was again, cleaning the ground-floor windows, and the ugly glass doors.

The security man seemed to have tired of pulling faces at her, and had buried himself in his newspaper again. Frustratingly, he was the only person she had seen all afternoon – no more delivery men had appeared round the back, not even a harassed suit had left the building. She knew nothing more than she had done last week.

She wished she knew what time it was. It was ages since they'd stopped for lunch. She was sure it must be nearly time to go home. Her dad was on the last side of the building, she was just finishing the front. She reckoned it would be another fifteen minutes, half an hour at most, and then they could leave. She just had to do the front doors and that would be it.

As she bent down to get some more water, her eye caught something moving inside the reception. It was speeding towards the oblivious security man from the end of a long corridor to his left. Millie peered down to ground level – it was coming towards the doors. It was moving too quickly for her to be sure – just a grey blur – but Millie was fairly certain that whatever was flying in her direction had four legs and a tail. As it approached the doors, she flipped the switch to open them. The security man still didn't look up – why would he? She had been mucking around with these doors for twenty minutes. The cat belted outside, and stopped so suddenly that dust flew up around it. It looked up at her appealingly.

'Hello,' Millie whispered, as the doors slid shut again.

'I'm sorry,' said the cat, 'there's really no time for pleasantries. Could you hide me, please, and we'll introduce ourselves properly later?'

Chapter Three

Millie jumped a clear six inches into the air. 'Wha—?' she struggled.

'There's no need to be so scared. I'm a cat, not your natural predator. You don't even *have* a natural predator. Well, maybe if you were in Kenya, and the lions were . . . Shh, there is no time for this.' He glared at her, as though she'd been the one talking. 'I am in a bit of a mess, so if you could help . . . Your jaw is hanging loose, by the way.'

'You can—'

'Talk, yes. How? It's a long story, one which I am, happily, well equipped to tell you, just not right now.' The cat was almost hissing now, looking behind him in alarm.

'Of course I can hide you.' Millie came to her senses, even if it was only temporarily. 'Here you go.' In one movement, she picked up her jumper, which was lying on the ground where she'd dropped it when the sun came out, and scooped up the cat, who sighed audibly. Millie ran over to the van and put her jumper and its contents on a pile of cleaning cloths in the back.

'Now go back to what you were doing,' muttered the cat. 'And whatever anyone asks you, lie.'

Millie ran back to the doors and picked up her cloth. She walked the last few paces, hoping that the security guard wouldn't think there was anything funny going on. She didn't normally go sprinting off for no reason, after all.

She was just in time. A few seconds later, a man came racing down the same corridor.

His legs flew out behind him, his lab coat swinging around him in all directions. He landed at the reception desk, panting heavily. Millie strained her ears, but she could hear nothing through the doors. She saw the security guard shake his head once, then again, more firmly. He listened for a minute, then jerked his head in Millie's direction. She tried to look very busy with her bucket. The cat's pursuer came rushing up to the doors, which wouldn't open.

'Hello? Hello?' he said, panicky.

'Hello.' Millie stared at him.

'The doors won't open,' he shouted, gesticulating wildly.

'No, I had to lock them,' Millie explained. 'The catch is just up here.' She released the doors. 'They're automatic. If I don't lock them, I can't wash the glass, can I? They just open.'

'How long have they been locked?'

Millie saw that the security guard was watching her

intently. The true answer was, 'About eight seconds, since I saw you coming.' The right answer was, 'The last ten minutes. Nothing has been able to get in or out in that time, not even a tiny fly. And I, by the way, have the same nasal condition as Pinocchio, so can't possibly be lying, or you'd be able to tell.' But the doors *had* opened, when she let the cat out – and the security man, even though he hadn't been looking, might have felt the breeze as they opened, mightn't he? It was a warm day, and not at all windy, but if she lied openly, she might get caught out. She hedged her bets and said, 'Dunno. A while.'

'How long?' he said again. There was a high note of hysteria in his voice.

'As long as it takes to do the doors.'

'How long has she been here?' The man had obviously given up on her as a surly teenager and was now quizzing the security guard.

'About half an hour?' he guessed. Millie nodded sullenly, delighted.

'The doors've been locked all that time?'

She nodded again, sure now that the security guard had been paying almost no attention at all.

'Damn it, he must've gone the other way . . .' The man started off back down the corridor. 'Lock the doors again, please. Now.' Millie shrugged and reached up to the switch. The security guard shrugged back at her and pulled a face, implying that this man was a bit odd. Millie frowned back at him, her expression a picture of puzzlement at what had just happened. He nodded and rolled his eyes, then went back to his newspaper. Excitement over.

She was safe.

Millie finished rinsing the window, not daring to hurry too much, in case the lab-coat man reappeared, and then carried her things back to the van.

'Are you all right?' she asked quietly, lifting her jumper off the cat.

'I smell of detergent. It wasn't a life-long aim. Otherwise I'm fine.'

'Is a man in a lab coat looking for you?' she asked.

'Yes. Did you put him off?'

'Yes. Your accent's funny. Where are you from?'

'A minute ago you couldn't believe I could talk. Now you're criticising my vowel sounds? That's quite picky, you know.'

'I wasn't criticising . . . I was interested.'

'You have a critical tone of voice, then.'

'Sorry,' said Millie, thinking the cat had a pretty critical tone himself at the moment.

'I'm from—'

'Stop! My dad's coming. Can you get in my bag?' Millie grabbed her bag from behind the seat.

'Do I have to?' begged the cat, looking with some disdain

at Millie's canvas rucksack, covered in stars, badges and ribbons.

'Yes,' said Millie firmly, pushing the cat into her bag, shoving her jumper on top, and flipping the catch shut, before spinning round to grin casually at her father and Bill as they wandered over to the van.

Chapter Four

'I'm going to do some stuff on the computer, Dad,' Millie shouted, as she ran ahead of him through the front door and flew up the stairs. She heard him say something as she shut the door behind her, but assumed that whatever it was, it could wait. Her wardrobe was right behind the door, and she opened it. This meant that if you tried to open the door to her room, it would bounce off the wardrobe door, and you couldn't walk immediately inside. It wasn't a very sophisticated system, but it provided a small level of cover for secrets and emergencies. Both of which seemed to describe the current state of affairs. She put her bag on the bed, opened it up and said, 'Hello again. You can come out now.'

'Finally,' sighed the cat, and angled his way past her jumper. 'I thought I was going to be in there for ever.'

'Sorry, we live quite a long way from the laboratory.'

'In the circumstances, I think that is a good thing. It was just a little bit small for such a long journey.' He looked back at the bag disapprovingly and stretched his spine. 'Is this your bedroom?' he asked, looking around him.

'Yup.'

'You have your own computer?' He seemed impressed.

'Yup.' Millie nodded. It was her prize possession.

'Good. So we could . . .' His voice tailed off, as he began to think.

'We could what?'

'Plan the escape of the others Monty, Celeste and everyone.'

'Sorry?'

The cat continued his train of thought: 'I mean, if we could—'

Millie decided she needed to reassert some control over this situation, which seemed to be looping out of her reach.

'Stop. Please.' The cat looked up at her and frowned. 'Could we start at the beginning? I'm Millie,' she said.

'Hello,' said the cat. 'I'm Max.' They looked at each other, and Millie held out a hesitant hand. Max reached up a front paw, and they patted each other, almost shaking hands.

'This is how you say hello in England, hmm? In Belgium, we would kiss three times on the cheek as well. It's friendlier, I think.'

'How did you end up here, if you're from Belgium?' Millie asked, wide-eyed. She would never have placed his accent if he hadn't told her. It was almost French, and almost something else, which she supposed must be Belgian. She thought he had a surprisingly low voice. Although she wondered exactly what tone of voice wouldn't be surprising, coming from a cat.

Max's eyes narrowed, as though he had just seen a larger and deservedly much less popular cat, perhaps with a limp and a missing eye, across the room. 'Kidnap,' he spat.

'Kidnap?' Millie sat down on the bed and crossed her legs.

'Exactly. I was roaming around Ixelles. That's near the Avenue Louise. In Brussels.'

'Where you used to live?'

'Where I still live,' he corrected her. 'I'm just not there at this exact moment. And it was around lunchtime, I guess, and I was thinking of finding something nice to eat, perhaps from the kitchen of one of the cafés—'

'You were going to steal lunch from a café?'

'Not *steal*. Liberate.'

'That's what my dad calls it.'

'He's a smart man. Anyway, I was just heading down a small alleyway to the back of La Perruche – my favourite café, where they serve some very good chicken – and I walked past a grey van. And as I was going past, a man threw something over me, a . . . I don't know the word in English. Like you use to catch fish.'

'A net?'

'Yes, a net. The humiliation. Caught like a stupid fish.'

'It's not that stupid.' Millie tried to console him. 'Being caught on a line would have been worse.'

'True.' Max nodded. 'Yes, that is a different level of stupid that only the fish can attain. "What is this that looks like a small meal, on a big sharp metal hook? I will, perhaps, just put my mouth around it and find out. That is surely the safest way to discover more. Ah! I am caught, who could have foreseen?" Everyone but the idiot fish, of course. No wonder they are becoming extinct. They deserve it.'

'I'm not sure that's *exactly* why they're becoming extinct,' Millie said, thinking that deep-sea fishermen probably almost never used fishing rods.

Max ignored her loftily. Some grievances couldn't be put aside, especially where fish were concerned.

'But this net is heavy, weighed down at the edges, so once it is over me, I can't get it off. And in an instant, I am lifted inside the van and put into a tiny box.'

'You must have been terrified,' Millie sympathised.

'Not terrified. Never terrified. Cats are very brave, you know. More angry, and unsure how to escape, and a little, you know, perhaps nervous.' He eyed her, warily, as he continued: 'That evening, I was shoved into a room full of cats in boxes. Next day, I was in a big car, with the windows blacked out, with another dozen or so cats. We were driven for a while, and then we went onto a boat.' Max shuddered, overcome by the distress of his kidnap, the memory of the long, cramped journey and the sheer fury of having been made to travel on water, when this was as unnatural to cats as flying through the air on wings.

'I saw that car!' Millie tried to keep her voice down, in case her dad could hear. 'Last week. There was an annoying man who had a couple of crates that—'

'That what?'

'That *meowed*,' she whispered.

'That would have been the most recent shipment. Another twelve stolen cats.'

'Miiiiilliiiiie!' her dad shouted up the stairs. 'Dinner time.'

'I'll be right there,' she called.

'I'll be right back,' she said to Max. 'Well, I'll be half an hour. Are you hungry? I'll bring you something up.'

'A little chicken, or maybe some fish would be nice.'

'Ah.'

'Ah?'

'I'm vegetarian. We probably don't have any meat in the house.'

'*No meat?*' Max looked as if she had just told him that, usually, she and her father wore cats' skins as coats, except for the nicest ones, which they used for matching hats.

'Well, *you* wouldn't like to be eaten.'

'That's true, but chickens are so stupid, and fish are so ugly. It's different, eating a carnivore – we are clever and—'

'Edible. It's an honour thing. Just because you *can* kill something, doesn't mean you should. Unless you don't have a choice. Like, if I was on a desert island or something, and I had to eat a fish or starve to death.' Millie frowned at this prospect, although the likelihood of it occurring anywhere in East Anglia seemed pretty slim.

'If we all thought that way,' Max sniffed, 'the world would be overrun with mice.'

Millie thought for a minute. 'OK. You catch mice, or birds, and eat them, fine. But humans don't need to do that. We can eat anything.'

'Interesting as these philosophical distinctions are, what *have* you got for me to eat?'

'Cheese?' Millie ventured.

'Cheese will do for now, thank you. But we will have to arrange something else tomorrow. I cannot live off cheese, like a cartoon mouse. I need amino acids that are only in meat.'

'You're pretty well informed, for a cat.'

'I've just spent three months in a laboratory – you pick things up.'

'Miiiiiilliiiiie!'

'I've got to go. I'll be back as soon as I can. If you hear anyone come up the stairs, hide under the desk in case it's not me.'

The cat looked plaintive. 'Make it a big piece of cheese. Maybe shape it like a sparrow. Or a goldfish. Even a squirrel.'

The door shut behind her, and the cat looked around his new home.

Chapter Five

Millie had the second largest bedroom in the house – her dad had the biggest one, 'because I'm the biggest', as he had unarguably pointed out when they moved in. And the smallest one was kept for 'visitors', who were usually Millie's friends. Max looked around him – he hadn't been in a girl's bedroom before. In Brussels, he lived with Sofie and her son, Stef, who must be about the same age as Millie, he guessed. But he had always thought that girls' rooms would look more, well, girly. Pink and so on. Millie's room was not like that at all. There were aerial photographs on the walls, some of the sea. He shuddered again. The walls were covered with lots of shelves filled with books. On her desk were a computer and printer, and some other devices he couldn't quite name. Maybe a scanner, he wondered, although he wasn't entirely sure what that was. Perhaps Sofie and Stef weren't very technologically minded, he thought, jumping up onto the desk and looking more closely at Millie's computer, which appeared to be both smaller and newer than the ones in the lab.

In many ways, the room matched its owner, Max decided. His rescuer had a very sensible face, but she definitely wasn't pretty. Although he would probably have tried to come up with a more flattering description, if pushed. Well, maybe not – cats have an obligation to tell the truth, even if they've just been assisted in a daring bid for freedom. Millie had dark brown hair, cut into what might generously be described as a mess. She wasn't very tall for her age, either, and she appeared to dress as though she were hoping to pass as a boy. He thought about how different she looked from the girls Stef knew. But the more he thought, the more he realised that it didn't matter – Millie could obviously think quickly in an emergency, and that was what he had needed most today, and would continue to need, if he was going to keep his promise to Monty.

Max blinked quickly. Some of the cats in the lab had been pretty boring, he thought. And one or two had been quite unpleasant, especially a big ginger tom who'd tried to bully Max when he first arrived. And then there was the cat who had stood up for Max, and refused to let anyone pick on him – Monty. He was the oldest cat in the lab, in his mid-teens. And his was the only family to have been kidnapped – Monty's daughter, Celeste, had been in the cage below Max, and they were the only cats that hadn't laughed at Max when he explained his plan to escape.

Max had promised them both that he would come back

and rescue them, as soon as he got the chance. The ginger tom had snorted with derision at the very idea that Max would make it to the outside world, let alone come back for his friends. Even Monty had only nodded sadly at Max, as though he couldn't quite believe that he would be able to do it. But, as Max had made his escape, Celeste had whispered, 'Come back for us, Max. We'll be waiting.' Max blinked at the memory and took a deep breath. He looked around approvingly at Millie's desk, with its supply of electronics, and began to plan.

Max had no idea how long he had been sitting, thinking, when he heard the telltale creak of a foot on the stairs. In less than a second he was under the bed. The door opened, and shut again quickly.

'Max?'

He wriggled out from under the bed, and sneezed twice, looking at Millie with an unmistakable air of reproach.

'Sorry,' she said guiltily. 'I always mean to hoover under there, but I usually forget. That's why I thought you might prefer hiding under the desk.'

'Yes,' he agreed ruefully.

'I brought you some cheese.'

'Thank you.'

'Now, tell me about the Haverham lab.'

'Is that what it's called?'

'No. Well, I don't know. It's just where it is. I don't know who owns it – I guess we could find out.' Millie jerked her head at the computer.

'Later, we will do that. First, I should tell you what they do there.'

'They're making cats that can talk.' Millie knew she was stating the obvious, but she was still having problems making her brain accept what her eyes and ears were telling her.

'Do you know why?' asked Max.

'Is it a government lab?' Millie's eyebrows shot up in alarm. 'Are you a secret weapon? Like a spy?'

'Yes, of course. Your government has decided it will send adorable kittens to dubious world leaders, media moguls and international terrorists. They will keep us on their laps at all times, because we are so furry and cute. We will overhear everything they plan, just like our role model, the fluffy white cat in your James Bond films. This has, in fact, been happening for many years, but with one flaw: we could not communicate what we knew. Many intelligence missions, many top-secret investigations, even many wars could have been avoided, if only we could tell what we had heard. And then, one day, *voilà*, someone has the bright idea. Kidnap cats from overseas, with a range of languages at their disposal. I, for example, speak French, Dutch and English, as you can hear. Give them voice-boxes, like humans have. Then, each time we go for our injections, or worm tablets, or minor operations, we can tell the vet everything we know, very, very quietly. The vet is not only a vet, but an operative from MI5. It is simple, but brilliant.'

Millie looked at Max for a long minute.

'You're pretty sarcastic for a cat.'

'No more than average. It's just you can hear me.'

'OK, it was a stupid suggestion. But who *does* have an interest in making animals talk?'

'I don't know. That is something we have to find out.'

'And do you know *why* they want to make cats talk? It might help us find out who's behind it.'

'No, they hardly let me see any memos while I was sitting in a cage.'

'You could just say no, you know.'

'Of course, but then how would you learn?' Max gazed at her innocently.

'Speaking of which, how have you learned so many languages so fast?'

'I have not learned them fast. Sofie, with whom I live in Brussels, is an English teacher. She helps her son, Stef, with his homework – he is around your age, I should think. They speak French and also Dutch at home – there are two national languages in Belgium, you know. Well, three, really, because everyone also learns to speak English. I have been able to understand all three languages for many years. Once I could speak at all, I could speak all the languages I knew. Pretty good, huh? You must be very jealous. Everyone knows that English people are hopeless at languages.'

Millie grinned, but they must have been talking too loudly to hear the stair creak, because an unexpected knock at the door made her leap suddenly to her feet.

Chapter Six

Max had dived back under the bed before Millie's dad's knuckles hit the door a second time. Millie was beginning to understand how the cat had escaped – he was astonishingly fast.

'Millie,' called her dad. 'Are you all right in there? Can I come in?' He had already begun to open the door. It banged immediately onto the open wardrobe door behind it. 'Oops, sorry.'

'I don't know why you bother asking, if you're just going to open the door anyway.' Millie sighed, trying to sound vaguely annoyed, while her heart pumped crazily. She jumped up to shut the wardrobe so that her dad could open the door properly.

'Sorry – I wasn't sure if you'd heard me over the TV.' He looked at the television, which was steadfastly switched off. 'That's funny, I could have sworn I heard—'

'What's up, Dad?' she asked brightly.

'Nothing, really, I just came to see if you were all right. You were so quiet at dinner, and you've been up here ever since we got home. You're upset because we were out at the lab today, aren't you?'

'Not exactly upset.' Millie didn't like fibbing to her father, and she was trying hard not to lie outright, but she could see it was going to be tricky.

'I know it bothers you, sweetheart. And I'm sorry I have to keep going there, but *you* don't, you know.'

'I know. I might not come out tomorrow, Dad, if you don't mind.'

'Well, we're not going back to Haverham lab till next week now anyway, so why don't you have a think about it?'

'I will. Do you, er . . .' Millie tried hard to be as unconcerned as possible. 'Do you happen to know who owns the laboratory?'

'No, I don't, love. A pharmaceutical company, I expect. That's what the protesters' signs all say.'

'I thought you hadn't seen any protesters? That man said they came quite late in the morning.'

'Well' – her dad looked a bit shame-faced – 'I saw them earlier, actually. I was looking out for them after you mentioned them the other day, and from the third floor you can just make out the main road, over the trees. I could see their banners, and a couple of them were big enough to read.'

'What did they say?' asked Millie curiously. Maybe this

was a chance to find out more about who had been kidnapping Max and the other cats.

'They were both the same – "The drugs don't work, and it's too high a price to pay".'

'It is, isn't it?' Millie was disappointed – she thought there would have been the name of a company at least.

'I can't answer that, sweetheart. We've been very lucky – it's easy for us to moralise. If you were ill, and needed new drugs to keep you alive and healthy, God forbid, all I know is that I prefer you to some rats in a cage.'

'What if it's not rats, though? What if it's a cat, or a dog, or a monkey?'

'Well, I wouldn't feel any differently. I still prefer you. But all animals are the same to me, love – I like them. I wouldn't hurt any of them by choice. You know that. I mean, I'd call a man in if we had mice running around the place, because they could start a fire, chewing through the wiring behind the walls. But a dog, a cat, a monkey, a guinea pig – none of them should live in a cage. That's why we don't keep a pet. Animals are wild creatures, they're not meant to be kept locked up.'

Even though she couldn't see him, Millie could feel Max nodding fervently.

'I know. But' – Millie had a sudden flash of brilliance – 'you wouldn't mind if I fed that cat that's been hanging around outside, would you?'

'Which cat?'

'The stray one I told you about.' This was a lie, but in such a good cause, she couldn't help herself. It was like telling someone they looked nice in a new but horrible dress to which they were irretrievably and inexplicably attached. Sometimes you had to lie for the greater good. After all, they wouldn't take the dress back if you said you didn't like it. They'd just like you slightly less for not lying to them.

'I don't remember,' her dad said, frowning slightly.

'I knew you weren't listening.'

'Well, don't get too attached to this cat – it almost certainly has a home somewhere else. Cats are pretty resourceful, you know. They don't often end up in a scrape.'

'He looks a bit skinny, Dad. Can I get him some cat food?'

'Well, I should think so. But cats can usually find their own food, you know. They don't very often go hungry.'

'Well, maybe this one's not been well. He looks a bit raggedy.' She heard a tiny, huffy hiss, which she hoped her dad wouldn't notice. 'I'll get some tomorrow. Thanks, Dad.'

'What are you up to now? Do you want to come and watch a film?'

'I'll be down in a minute.'

Her dad recognised his cue to leave. 'OK. I'll just go and make a couple of calls – I've been meaning to do them all week. Come down when you're done up here.'

The door shut behind him. Millie went and opened the

wardrobe secondary defence again. Max appeared from under the bed.

'I hope he's not ringing that woman,' Millie said thoughtfully. Max didn't hear.

'*Raggedy?*' was all he could say, almost spitting.

'Not really,' she said quickly. Cats' feelings were obviously more easily wounded than she had imagined.

'I just needed to have a reason to buy you some food,' she explained.

'Well, that was pretty quick thinking, I suppose,' he congratulated her.

'Thanks. You're going to have to try and look a bit scrawnier, though.'

'Scrawnier?'

'Thinner.'

'What are you saying? I am a very handsome cat. I am a Chartreux, from the ancient French cat family.'

'Exactly.' Millie smiled. She couldn't deny that Max was a beautiful cat. He had thick blue-grey fur, and extraordinary, almost glowing orange eyes. 'You're supposed to look like some skanky stray who needs feeding. So if I were you, I'd groom a bit less, and maybe try and flatten your fur down, so you look smaller and more pathetic.'

'Pathetic? I have never heard such a thing. I will catch birds myself and eat those.'

'There might be times when I can't let you outside, when

my dad's here. Then what are you going to do? It's either look a bit feeble on the off chance my dad or the lady next door sees you, or a diet of cheese. You decide.'

Max thought for a moment. 'You are right,' he said, defeated. 'I shall try hard to look . . . ordinary. It won't be easy.'

Chapter Seven

The next day, Millie told her dad that she would stay at home – there was a book she wanted to finish before she had to take it back to the library. No problem, he had said cheerily, he'd drop a note round next door, and Mrs Ellis, their neighbour, could pop by and see she was OK. Millie rolled her eyes heavenwards, and asked again what an old lady would be able to do if the much-heralded crisis ever actually occurred, perhaps swim in to rescue her if a water main burst, for example. Her dad told her not to be so ungrateful and ruffled her hair, in a way which was designed to be only slightly annoying, as he left.

Millie opened the door to the back garden, and let Max out of her room. He flew off, delighted by the prospect of some real, undiluted freedom for the first time in many weeks. He was keen to start planning the rescue of the other cats as soon as they possibly could, but they both agreed that he should have a look around Millie's neighbourhood first, and stretch his legs. How else would he get in shape for a mission?

Millie found her book and read it, lying on a towel on the grass, waving up at Mrs Ellis when she saw her, to try and put her off coming round and interfering. Max reappeared an hour later, looking sleek and happy, with the merest trace of feathers around his mouth. Millie got up casually and wandered into the kitchen, as though she were going to get something to drink. She really, really didn't want Mrs Ellis to think she had seen her talking to a mysterious cat. Max snuck in through the French windows.

'I can see what you've been eating,' Millie said, wrinkling her nose in disgust.

'If they only came with napkins . . .' Max shrugged. He licked his lips. 'Now let's go and do some proper hunting,' he said.

They went back upstairs, and were online a few moments later, looking for the protesters' website. They soon found a page which explained that the Haverham laboratory belonged to Vakkson, a pharmaceutical company with offices in London, France, Germany and Spain. The laboratory was their only one in the UK, but they had several more on the Continent. The protesters claimed that the reason the company went largely unnoticed was because they 'only tested on rodents, which aren't cute enough to stir up public feelings. People would react differently if it was puppies they were torturing.'

'*Some* people would react differently,' muttered Max.

'Don't be so unkind,' Millie said hotly. 'Just because you don't like dogs.'

'I don't like rodents either,' he pointed out. 'Except as a starter.'

'These people are on our side, you know. They're the ones trying to stop Vakkson from testing on animals. I think they stand outside all day with placards and shout at all the cars that come onto the property.'

'Have you seen them?' Max asked, interested.

'No. They get there after we do. My dad saw them, though, over the trees.'

'So, how have they helped, exactly?'

'Maybe they haven't. But at least they're trying.'

'I suppose so. But they obviously know very little about what's been going on, if they think there are only mice and rats in there. I presume even quite a stupid person would realise I am not a mouse. Or a grubby little rat.'

'And they think that it's only medicines that are being tested. But that's not what they were using you for, is it?' Millie frowned.

Max had no idea. He shrugged.

'I mean,' Millie carried on, trying to explain, 'they didn't give you a voice to test a medicine, unless it was an unexpected side-effect, which doesn't seem very likely. I can imagine there are medicines which could *damage* your voice, but not give you one from scratch. And they don't need to find a medicine that can make people talk – we can talk already.'

'More's the pity,' snapped Max. 'Present company excepted of course. You're right, though. So, what *were* they doing?'

'I don't know. Maybe I'm wrong – *could* it have been a side-effect of a drug? Did they seem surprised when they found you could talk?'

'Not as surprised as you did.'

Millie grinned. 'I bet they didn't. So they expected you to be able to talk?'

'Yes. I think so. They asked us questions. That suggests that they were expecting answers.'

'When did they ask you questions?' Millie asked.

'Every day.'

'From the day you arrived there?'

'No, from the second or third day. I'm not sure. I was tired, and my throat hurt.' Max looked a bit dejected, not something Millie had seen before.

'Your throat hurt? Let me see.' Millie reached out for his neck, and he jumped back, hissing.

'I'm sorry,' Millie cried, and pulled back her hand as if scalded. They looked at each other for a long moment.

Max sighed.

'No, *I* am sorry. I know you're trying to help me, and I didn't mean to get angry. It's just—'

'I know,' she said, imagining how she might feel if the last human being to come near her had kidnapped and tortured her. 'I just want to see if there are marks on your fur.'

He stepped forward, and she put her hand gently on his throat, where the fur seemed shorter than elsewhere. She nodded, grimly.

'I think you were tired because they gave you an anaesthetic the day after you arrived. And your throat hurt because while you were unconscious, they operated on you to give you a voice. Your fur's shorter here, because they must have shaved it. I had my tonsils out last year, and my throat hurt for a fortnight. And yours must have been much worse than that.'

Max looked a bit sick.

'They . . . shaved my fur?' he said faintly.

'Yes, I think so.'

'Tell me we will punish them for this indignity,' he said.

'Of course we will. Do you always sound like one of the Three Musketeers when you get angry?'

'Always.'

They sat for a moment, and Millie gave him a small smile.

'Did they test you for any other things?'

'They took temperatures, heart rates, that kind of thing. They had charts on each of us, I think,' he replied.

'That just sounds like they wanted to check whether the surgery had made you ill in any way. Did they operate on all the cats as soon as they came in?'

'I guess so. I don't know exactly.' Max furrowed his brow, trying to remember.

'Could you all talk, in the end?'

'Yes. Although they thought one of us could not.'

Millie raised her eyebrows, questioning.

Max explained: 'There was one cat, Monty, who refused to talk to them at all. He could, but he wouldn't. He was there when I arrived, and he was very smart, very funny. He took care of me. He was always planning some kind of escape, but he is old and not so quick or strong as I am. His daughter, Celeste, was there too – he was planning for her, I think . . .' Max gazed at Millie. 'We *must* help them.'

'We will,' said Millie simply. 'I promise.'

'After the first couple of days, when they started questioning us, he never answered. They thought it hadn't worked on him.'

'The surgery?' asked Millie.

'Yes, the surgery. They spoke to us all, and we all replied. It didn't occur to us not to, you know, when we found we could talk. We wanted to ask them where we were, what they'd done to us, when we could leave.'

'And did you?'

'Of course, but they never replied. Just told us to be quiet.'

'How ironic.'

'Quite. Anyway, Monty never replied to any of their questions, although I think he'd been through the same operation as the rest of us. They were very annoyed about it. They did more tests on him than on all the rest of us put together. He just used to yowl at them, like a normal cat.'

'And he *could* talk, he just wouldn't?'

'Yes.' Max suddenly sounded tired.

'I'm sorry,' Millie said, 'I know you probably don't want to think about it very much.'

'Quite the contrary. If it helps us to rescue my friends, I will think about it all day. What do *you* think was happening?'

'I think they wanted to give you all voices. That must have been the plan. I just can't think why.'

Chapter Eight

Millie and Max spent the next hour online, trying to find out as much as they could. There were two sites in particular which interested them – the first was the initial one they had looked at, which complained about Vakkson and its rodent testing, and had as its address *www.haverhamlabprotest.co.uk*. The second Millie found by searching again, and it came up as *www.haverhamlabprotest.org*.

'That's weird,' said Millie. 'Why would there be another one?'

Max had no sensible suggestions to make. He wasn't much of an internet expert, he admitted, and didn't really know what to make of it all. Millie clicked onto the link, and went to look at the second site, which seemed fairly similar in content to the first. She combed through it, trying to see why someone had set up a second site. There was a diary page and she clicked onto that.

'Maybe this will help,' she said, beginning to read. 'Ah.'

'Ah?' said Max. He had been hoping for less reading and more action, and though he could see that Millie thought this was all useful research, he was getting a little bored. He'd thought that perhaps they could just run to the lab and get the others out today, although he did admit that this plan lacked sophistication.

'They've fallen out with each other,' she explained, pointing to the screen. It appeared that the protesters had now formed two groups: one who did the placards and shouting, and one who thought the first lot a bunch of wimps, and advocated 'direct action'.

'What do you think that means?' asked Max.

'Rescue missions?' guessed Millie.

'Really?'

'No, probably not. Well, maybe. I think they do that sometimes. But usually I think they do things like hassle the people who work for the lab, and their families, and stuff. Try to frighten them out of doing it.'

'Seems fair,' said Max.

'Mmm,' said Millie.

'You don't think so?' he asked, surprised.

'I don't know,' she replied. 'I met some people last year who were campaigning against animal testing labs. And I wanted to join them, but some of them were really scary, and Dad wouldn't let me.'

'What do you mean, scary?'

'I mean, they would ring the people who worked at the lab in the middle of the night . . .'

'That's not so bad,' said Max.

'. . . and threaten to kill their children,' she finished.

'Oh. That's not so good,' he admitted. 'Still, they started it, kidnapping cats.'

'I know, but their kids aren't to blame, are they?'

'No. I suppose not.' Max didn't look entirely convinced.

'Maybe we should get in touch with the first lot,' said Millie.

'But if we are going to try and rescue the others, that's direct action, is it not?' asked Max.

'Yes. I guess so.' Millie thought for a moment. 'There aren't any phone numbers or other contact details. Let's mail them both. We'll see what we can find out.'

'No, don't do that.' Max stood up suddenly. 'What if they are not real people, writing these things?'

'You think fictional people are doing it? Can they even type?'

Max gave Millie a long, level stare. 'Not fictional people, Miss Clever,' he said, making her smirk. 'You might wish to remember,' he added haughtily, 'that I am speaking in my third language. I *mean*, what if the people at the laboratory are behind the sites? They are not real protesters, even though they are real people.'

'Calm down,' said Millie. 'I'm on it. I'm going to set up a

special account, which is remote from this computer. We'll mail them from there, and they won't be able to track it back to us at all. And we'll only use it for mailing this site, so nobody will be able to put two and two together.'

'Why would they do that?'

'It's just an expression – put two and two together. It means take little bits of evidence and jump to a big conclusion. But they won't be able to match the person mailing the site with the girl cleaning windows. I promise.'

Max still looked sceptical, but eventually shrugged his consent.

'Now,' Millie continued, 'we need a user name, and a password – something no one else would know.' She picked up her book, flipped to a random page, and picked the first two nouns – overcoat and collar – that she found on page 35. 'Right, that's it. The username is "overcoat1", and the password is "collar35". *We'll* remember that, but no one would be able to guess it.'

'That's pretty clever,' said Max. 'Have you done this kind of thing before?'

'My dad's really interested in codes and ciphers,' replied Millie. 'He wrote computer programs before he lost his job. He's nuts about stuff like this. He's always going on about how people use stupid stuff for passwords – their friend's name, or their pet's, and their birthday, or someone they know's birthday, you know, for the number. Makes it easy for someone else to guess. But if you open a book at random, and pick two words, no one is going to guess those. Even if they get the book you were reading, what are the chances they'll come to the same page that you did, and pick out the same words?'

'So, how will *you* remember them?' asked Max, confused.

Millie shrugged. 'I just will,' she replied. 'How do you remember your way around Ixelles?'

Max nodded slowly.

'Right, that's the account set up,' Mille continued. 'Now, the message.'

> hello – i am mailing to ask you about the haverham lab. i've been reading your site, and you seem to think that they only have rodents there. i am sure there are also cats being used for tests in that building. i want to expose the truth. can you help me?

'That should do, don't you think?'

'I suppose so,' Max agreed. 'We don't want to expose the truth straight away, though. We need to get the others out first, especially Celeste and Monty.'

'I know. But we'll have to offer them something, or they might not reply.'

'OK, send it.' Max was suddenly decisive.

Millie pressed the button. They waited for the ticking arrow to turn. *Message sent* flashed up on the screen. She did it again, and sent the same message to the second site.

'Now what?' asked Max.

'Now I take this book back to the library and get you some cat food. You go for a wander, if you want to, or stay here, if you don't. I'll be back in an hour and we can see if they've replied.'

Chapter Nine

Max decided to go and lie in the sunshine in Millie's back garden. He had been warned by Millie about the nosy neighbour, so he found a tree to hide under and he lay behind it, watching the stupid, stupid birds, and wondering about another meal. There were insects buzzing all around him and he thought about catching one of those, just for the practice. At this point, a butterfly flapped into his ear and he sneezed. Probably there wasn't much point trying to catch something that would just fly into you anyway. He lounged in the sun and began to snooze.

Millie, meanwhile, waved cheerily at Mrs Ellis as she went out of the front door. She explained that she was just off to the library and showed her a bag full of books. This was such an unquestionably respectable errand that Mrs Ellis waved back and didn't interfere at all. Millie swapped her books for a new batch with only half her mind on the job. When she got home, she would realise that she had read two of them before. She stopped off at the supermarket and bought dry cat food for Max, because the tins were much too heavy to carry. Then she saw some little pouches of special cat food and bought one as a treat. She chose a cake for herself, so Max wasn't the only one eating something nice, and hurried home. She unlocked the French windows, but before she had even opened them fully, Max was snaking around her feet.

'You must have sonar.' Millie laughed. 'Did the key make that much noise?'

'Ah, it's nothing. Everyone has something they are good at. Not all cats hear well, you know. There's a cat near my home who is quite deaf. He will get hit by a car some day, and it will be very sad. On the other hand, if your hearing is bad, it's not so sensible to sit in the middle of the road.'

'I brought presents. Look.' Millie showed Max the dry cat food and the special pouch. 'This was expensive, so I only got you one. But I'll get you some more if it's nice. I wasn't sure if you liked the dry stuff.'

'You know, you are a very kind girl. And I will enjoy it, I am sure. I might still supplement it with the occasional bird or fish, however.'

'Max, don't steal fish from the goldfish pond next door but one. I'll get in trouble.'

'Really?'

'Well, I will if they see you lying next to me in the middle of our garden and realise I'm the one who's responsible for you.'

'I am responsible for myself.'

'Yes, well, you can tell my dad that when they come round demanding to know why we're looking after a cat who visibly isn't a stray and letting it eat fish out of their pond. They're really mean, that family.'

'Very well. It is OK to eat their canary?'

'That's not even a bit funny.'

'If they had had a canary, it would have been hilarious.'

'Shush. Now, come on. Let's go and check if we've got any new messages.'

Millie logged onto their new account. 'Inbox: 2 new messages', it read. She clicked on the first, which came from the first website.

> hi. how do you know what's going on there? do you work there? we haven't seen any deliveries of cats in the last six months, since the campaign began. will try to find out more.

'They think we work there. This is great.' She typed back:

> i used to work there. not in the laboratory part. the cats are delivered at the back – that's how they get them in without you seeing. do you know who would be behind the testing? or how I could find out?

She pressed 'Send' and a reply arrow appeared next to the

mail she'd received. They waited in silence for a few seconds, and Millie was just about to click on their other mail, when a new mail flashed back up.

> the lab is run by vakkson, so testing probably
> being carried out by them. will look into this
> further. thanks for the tip.

'And now we wait?' asked Max.

'Yes, I think so. Let's look at our other mail.' As Millie expected, it came from the *.org* protesters. Max was having some problems remembering who was who. She clicked on the second mail and read:

> cats as well? do you want to do something
> about it?

'What shall I put?' she said, looking at the cat.

'Say yes,' he suggested.

'OK.' She typed:

> yes, we do. will you help?

The reply came back immediately:

> yes. keep me posted.

'That looks promising,' said Millie, as she logged out of the account. 'Let's look for any more information we can find about the laboratory online. My dad's not going back there until next week, so we can't find anything out from the building until then. Maybe I can try and find some more stuff here.'

'We can't do things any . . . faster?' asked Max despondently.

'I don't think so,' Millie apologised. 'I know we need to help your friends. But I think we need to know more before we can rescue them. It's going to be difficult.'

'And dangerous.' Max nodded.

The Net search proved fruitless. The keywords 'Haverham laboratory' and 'Vakkson' only ever took them to animal rights protest pages, or angry chat-rooms where people debated the pros and cons of animal testing.

'I'm sorry, Max. I think we will have to wait for these guys to get back to us. Or for next week, when I can go out there with dad and see what I can find out.'

They sat, disconsolate, in the garden – Millie eating her cake and Max rolling grumpily on the lawn. Neither of them had the slightest idea that Millie's dad and Bill had already received a phone call from the lab, asking if they could go back the next day for some extra cleaning work. And Millie's dad, of course, had no idea when he agreed that the man who had telephoned him couldn't have cared less about the state of the windows. He was just sure that one of the window cleaners must have seen his missing property and was determined to find out who knew exactly what.

Chapter Ten

Arthur Shepard hadn't ever intended to be what his children, had they known what his job entailed, would certainly have described as 'a bad man'. He had never been especially clever, and he had never worked especially hard, but the main reason he'd ended up with the life he had was because he didn't especially care. About anybody, except Arthur Shepard. He had seemed to, briefly, at various times in his life – for example, in job interviews, or when he met the woman he would later, only half-interested in the response, ask to marry him, or when his children, whose names he could only sporadically remember, were born.

This was very much the pattern of his life: he didn't work, as he claimed, to provide for his wife and children; he worked to get away from them. If a lie detector had been taped to his forehead and he had been asked if he loved his family, he would have said yes, and it would have registered nothing. Arthur Shepard genuinely thought he loved his family, because he had no idea what other people meant by the term 'love'.

But the truth was that if someone had asked him if he would rather see his children ill or be ill himself, see his wife unhappy or be unhappy himself, he would always, always have chosen for them to suffer, and to remain unhurt himself. He wasn't ashamed of this, because he didn't realise that someone else might answer the same question differently.

Nonetheless, Arthur had never expected to end up doing what he did now. He had moved from job to job over the years, and when he had begun to work for Vakkson, he hadn't had any misgivings about a company with such a poor record in welfare and research. It was simply a well-paid job. When this particular scheme had presented itself to him, he hadn't hesitated before seizing the opportunity with outstretched hands. The only problems that he had been able to see had been practical: where would they find the cats, where would they keep them, how would they transport them in secrecy, how could they avoid the prying eyes of the bleeding hearts campaigning, if you could call it that, outside the front gate. As each problem was resolved, Arthur Shepard felt the buzz of a job well done. The rights and wrongs of it simply never occurred to him.

In the first place, he had realised that they would need a reasonable number of cats for the development stage – several hundred, in fact. They couldn't breed them, because cats take too long to mature – they didn't have months to sit around waiting for gambolling kittens to become adult cats. It would have to be theft. He had also realised that if they stole them all from the Haverham area, the ensuing cat drought would not go unremarked by residents. Even if his staff broadened their search to the rest of the country, they ran the risk of being seen and traced to the laboratory. The most sensible thing was to do it abroad, in a rented van, and keep as much distance between the project and the outside world as possible. Belgium had been the ideal place to start – barely any distance from Calais and the Eurotunnel and car-ferries. The men transported the cats a dozen at a time – none of them was ever stopped, but if they had been, it would have been such a minor offence, they would not have been in much trouble. The transport had been easy to arrange: transfer the cats from the van to a car – customs were on the lookout for large-scale cigarette and alcohol smuggling, or illegal immigrants – they had no interest in a small car with tinted windows that contained only a few crates.

And, of course, his masterstroke had been to avoid any real harassment from the protesters, because Arthur Shepard owned them. Two men and three women were paid by him to keep the protest happening, so no real protesters could feel it was a cause no one cared about and decide to get involved, like the meddling idiots they were. These employees (he liked to think of them as moles, as he had always had a faint interest in spying) ran a mildly critical website, which copied everything that came into it to him. He believed there had been some sort of argument with a few meddling idiots, who'd decided that his moles were insufficiently committed to their cause, and had set up a rival website, but it was so small-scale that it caused him no real anxiety. Everything was running smoothly. Until yesterday.

Yesterday, he had *not* felt the buzz of a job well done. He had felt the queasy panic of a job mucked up. The technician who had been in charge of the cats was already in a great deal of trouble, and if Arthur could have fired him he would have, immediately, as an example to the others. But the problem with that was that the project was top secret, obviously, and the man was a great deal more dangerous to Arthur *outside* of the laboratory, where he might say something to somebody, than *inside*, where he would be sterilising Petri dishes for the next five years. The cat had escaped, which was infuriating and risky. But, more worryingly, it had escaped when there were outsiders on the property – those stupid window cleaners. If only Vakkson hadn't hired them to keep the building clean. Any one of them could have seen something, and one of them probably had. Arthur felt no compunction as he rang them. He felt no guilt as he lied to the man to get them back there the next day. He simply took the opportunity to try and sort things out so that his cover wasn't blown, his contract wasn't terminated, he and several of his colleagues weren't arrested, and he continued, as he expected, to be on the verge of making tens of millions of pounds.

Chapter Eleven

Millie could hardly believe her luck. Her dad had come home from work, explaining that there was an extra shift at the Haverham lab and that they had arranged to do it the very next day. However, she was also puzzled: they had surely cleaned every window the day before. But, it transpired, the lab had cleaning staff who looked after the doors and windows inside the building, while Millie, her dad and Bill cleaned the outside. There had been some sort of staff shortage, and so they were being called back to do some additional work. Millie had said she would probably come and help, trying not to make her dad suspicious by being too eager. She wandered off upstairs to find Max.

'I might get some answers sooner than we thought – we've been asked to go back to the lab tomorrow,' she said, closing the door behind her.

'What? Why?'

'Windows need cleaning *indoors*, apparently.'

'Has this ever happened before?' Max asked.

Millie shook her head. 'No . . . I don't think so. Why?'

'It could be a trap, don't you think? They might think you have seen something.' Max paced worriedly up and down her bedroom floor.

'Hmmm. Maybe. They didn't ask for me to go, though. Just Dad and Bill.' Millie tried to weigh up the possibilities.

'But they cannot ask for you, of course. It would be too suspicious.'

'I suppose so,' Millie agreed. It wasn't very likely that they would book some window cleaners and ask them to bring a twelve-year-old girl with them. It would sound, at best, dodgy. 'Do you think I shouldn't go? Dad will be there. And Bill. And we'll be inside the building – I might be able to find something out that would help us.'

'That's true.' Max continued to pace. 'I think, though, that it will be a risk for you to go tomorrow. Are you sure you want to?'

'How else will we find out who's doing this?' Millie couldn't see any alternative.

'I know. But you must be prepared for people to ask you questions,' Max warned her.

'That man asked me questions as soon as you'd escaped, and I was OK,' she pointed out.

'Millie, I know. I am not doubting your abilities. I just want you to remember that these men do not have the same ideas as you about what is right and what is wrong. If they're willing to kidnap crate-loads of cats, they may not think twice about kidnapping, or even hurting, a little girl.'

'I'm not little. And I won't be on my own.'

'Maybe I should come with you,' he suggested.

Millie's eyes popped. 'Are you insane? You just escaped. I can't deny having seen you if your tail is poking out of my bag, can I?'

'No. I suppose not. I don't want to go back, of course, but I don't want you to have to go on your own either.' He looked decidedly unhappy.

'I'll be fine. I'll be with Dad. They can't kidnap me – he'd notice. Probably before he and Bill got back here, even.' He gave her a small smile. 'This is a chance to get a proper look inside.'

Max gave in.

'Then we will make a plan, yes? I will show you where you need to be looking.'

'Done.' Millie was relieved they'd managed to avoid having a fight. 'What am I looking for?'

'Do you have a pen?'

'Yes, why?'

'To draw a map, from what I tell you.' Millie pulled a quizzical face. He went on, 'You will have noticed, of course, that although I have a fine speaking voice, I am not yet at the point where I have opposable thumbs.'

She nodded. 'Sorry.'

*

Between them, they sketched out a good working plan of the building. It was a large oblong block, three storeys high, and Max knew he had come down three flights of stairs to the lobby, so they assumed that he had been on the third floor – the top-most one. Millie knew there were two staircases: the one which Max had raced down, and one in the opposite corner of the building, because she had cleaned the windows around them just yesterday. Max had only seen what looked like office or cup-board doors as he raced along the top corridor, unlike the glass-fronted doors of the laboratory, so they guessed that the researchers might work up on that floor too. Neither of them knew what went on on the second floor. Millie guessed that might be where the rodent research took place – the official pur-pose of the laboratory building. Max wasn't convinced that there were any mice in the building at all. They knew no more about the first floor; probably more offices, Millie thought. The ground floor, which she knew best, having looked in through its windows several times, housed cleaning cupboards, the big lobby and its jungle of pot plants, plus one other room that Millie couldn't quite remember. She must have looked glumly through its windows a dozen times, but she just couldn't quite place what it was. Eventually, she gave up trying, and they agreed that her plan of action was simple: clean what she was asked to clean, and don't look too interested but pay attention to anything she saw, in case it was useful. Don't attract anybody's notice. That was it.

*

Millie told her dad that she'd come with him tomorrow, and he had been pleased, if surprised. Max had decided to spend the night outdoors and would turn up again the next afternoon for a report. So everything was settled quite easily and Millie gave the whole thing very little thought, which was a shame, because if she had thought for a few more minutes, she wouldn't have been in Bill's van, turning into the driveway of the Haverham lab, before she remembered that the far wall of the forgotten room on the ground floor, opposite the window, was taken up by a huge bank of television screens, connected to CCTV cameras, which covered the whole building – including, of course, the front doors.

Milli and her dad [illegible] clear with the [illegible], and he [illegible] pleased [illegible] Mrs. [illegible] to [illegible] the [illegible] [illegible] quite early and Milli [illegible] [illegible] the [illegible] [illegible]

Chapter Twelve

Millie felt sweat bead on her forehead. How could she have been so stupid? This was a scientific laboratory, the chances were it contained drugs. There was a security man in the lobby, and the building was patrolled by more of them at night – she'd seen them arriving early for a shift once. The research the lab carried out was controversial at best, and had attracted the attention of a band of determined and angry protesters. Any one of these reasons was enough for the building to be covered in cameras. How could she have thought otherwise? Even if she had never been there, even if she hadn't seen the cameras, spinning slowly and silently around to keep a check on what she was doing, she should've realised. She was such an idiot. Of course they knew about Max's escape – they would have seen a tape of the whole thing. This was a trap. Max had been right all along. She wondered if they'd called the police. Had she stolen Max, if they had stolen him in the first place? So maybe they couldn't call the police. But the cats had been stolen abroad, if Max was anything to go by, and that might not count. How would the police in Haverham know about a spate of Belgian cat thefts?

These thoughts fizzed around in Millie's head, as her dad and Bill unpacked the van, filled the buckets, and went inside to find out where they were to start. The security man was the same one who'd been there on Tuesday, and he smiled at Millie. She felt a little better as she smiled back. He wouldn't be smiling if he knew what she'd done, surely. Unless it was deliberate, and he was trying to put her off her guard . . .

After an hour of cleaning the inside of the windows she'd cleaned only two days before on the outside, she began to wish someone *would* come and start shouting at her, just so the endless waiting would be over.

As it happened, she didn't have much longer to wait. A woman came out through the nearest stairwell and said something to her dad. He nodded, looking surprised, and followed her. Five minutes later, the same woman approached Bill, and he too disappeared. Millie looked over at the security man. He smiled again.

'Everyone's leaving you to do all the work today, huh?' he said. 'That happens to me all the time.'

'I wonder where they've gone,' Millie said, hoping she didn't sound as desperate as she felt.

'There's probably some other things that need cleaning

upstairs. Doors and windows and such. With the cleaners on strike, everything is getting messed up – the windows are dirty, the rubbish is piling up—'

'Oh, are they on strike? No wonder. The windows down here are massive – they probably got sick of cleaning them.' Millie sounded so boring she was embarrassed. But she was desperate to keep the conversation going to try to find out more.

'Well, you should know, darling, you do them every week. And yes, on strike. Well, not exactly. They have been . . .' he looked exaggeratedly from left to right '. . . got at.'

'Got at?' asked Millie, confused.

'Terrorised. The protesters, you know.'

'No, what did they do?'

'They threatened to take the cleaners' pets from their homes while they are here.'

'Really?' said Millie, thinking that this sounded extremely appropriate, given what had happened to Max. Still, she reminded herself, the *cleaners* hadn't kidnapped him, had they? It was a bit hard on them to start pinching their dogs or gerbils – they were only cleaning, after all.

'Yes. And the cleaners have walked out. They are not coming back until they are allowed to bring their pets to work.'

'Er . . .' Millie was at a loss for words. Did this man know she'd removed Max from the lab? Was that why he was saying all these things about taking pets that seemed designed to prick her guilty conscience? He looked so friendly, though – could he be so sneaky?

'How come they haven't threatened you?' she asked, determined to find out more, even if she was being lied to.

'They don't know who I am,' he explained softly. 'And' – he looked around again – 'I have fooled them. I don't have a pet!' He exploded with laughter, as if this was the best joke he'd ever heard. Millie smiled politely.

'So, no one's doing the cleaning?' she asked, trying to get back to the subject of the laboratory.

'Nope. Just you today. I would help you, you know, but I have to answer the phones.' Millie nodded understandingly. The phones had never rung while she'd been in earshot.

'Cleaning windows is less boring than sitting at a desk all day,' she said. She had found that most adults, except for her dad when he had had his computer job, spent a fair amount of time thinking they had a worse job than anybody else they knew, so she reckoned this was a good conversation-maker. But the security man seemed unusually happy with his lot.

'Well, I'm sure that's true. But don't you go feeling sorry for me. There's some guys here have to do the night shift every week, wandering about every evening when it's cold and dark, with dogs and torches.'

'But some guys get to sit around watching CCTV screens all day. That must be the best job, surely?' Millie couldn't believe she was saying this. Maybe she should just hold out her hands and tell him she'd done it.

The security man's eyebrows shot up to his hairline. 'How'd you hear about that?' he whispered.

'Oh, I've just seen the screens, you know, through the windows,' Millie answered, thinking that if they were supposed to be a secret, they should shut the blinds. And maybe disguise the cameras as really boring gargoyles.

'Oh. I thought you meant Lance. You didn't mean Lance?'

'Who's Lance?'

'He's a buddy of mine. He got fired yesterday.'

'Oh, I'm sorry.' Millie's insides were now twisting like a phone cable.

'It's not your fault, darling,' he reassured her. Millie hoped this man didn't know that it almost certainly *was* her fault. Well, hers and Max's.

'It was his own doing,' the security man said irritably. 'I told him a hundred times not to spend the day watching the wrong kind of TV. He just didn't want to hear it.'

'What's the wrong kind of TV?' Millie asked.

'Well, our cameras only record things at night, you see.' He gesticulated at the camera nearest them both, to illustrate his point. 'During the day, they just show what's happening right now. They don't store the images, and the film gets wiped over straight away, because otherwise we would have hundreds of tapes of people who work here coming in and out, and doing their jobs, and nothing else. We don't have room for all those tapes. The screens show what we call a live feed all day, so if someone runs towards the building holding a big round bomb, marked "BOMB", we see them coming.'

He paused and looked down kindly at Millie. 'That isn't going to happen, by the way.'

She guessed she must look as bad as she felt, if he believed that the thought of cartoon bombers made her pale with fear.

'So the tapes only get kept from overnight,' he finished.

'Uh huh.' Millie thought she might actually be sick. Could it be that they didn't have a record of Max sneaking into her bag? And that only one person might have seen it? So it would just be her word against someone else's?

'So, Lance is the one who is supposed to watch the cameras, keeping an eye on everything. But it *is* a boring job, you know, sitting in a room all day on your own, watching pictures of the building with nothing happening. You and your *colleagues*' – he said the word with an annoying emphasis, like they weren't really her colleagues because she was just a kid – 'were the highlight of his week. Some people to watch, for a change.'

'Oh, right.' She nodded. This was so unlucky. The man with the world's dullest job had been watching her just because he had literally nothing else to watch. He *must* have seen her, then.

The security man continued, oblivious: 'Only, I guess you lot have been coming too long, and he's not interested in you any more, either.'

'What do you mean?'

'I mean, he wasn't watching the cameras this week. He was watching TV. He'd brought in a little aerial, and he was watching *Murder, She Wrote* when one of the big bosses came in to ask him a question. You know *Murder, She Wrote*? The one where the lady detective writer goes around solving crimes, and there is a new murder every day, and no policeman ever says, "You know what? I think it is you who is murdering everyone, and then bamboozling people with your detective books. I think they are a smokescreen for you being the most successful serial killer ever. You are under arrest. And do not threaten me with a new book, because it will not work! You will be in prison, where you belong – and you will not have a typewriter!"'

Millie was getting more and more bemused, but she nodded encouragingly. He obviously felt strongly about this.

'So Lance is out on his ear. No references, nothing. So you and me should be getting on with our work, in case the same thing happens to us.'

'Yes, absolutely.' Millie smiled at the man with relief and delight. She turned back to the window. They hadn't seen her, because the man had been watching a murder mystery and not the front door. There wasn't a tape, because it was immediately recorded over. She might have got away with it after all.

'Excuse me, Millie?' A woman was standing right behind her and Millie jumped about three feet in the air.

'Sorry, I didn't mean to scare you.'

'You didn't,' Millie lied. 'I just didn't hear you come up behind me.'

'I'm Elaine, Mr Shepard's secretary. I was wondering if I could ask you a couple of questions. Would you come with me?'

'Sure.' Millie smiled without sincerity, hoping it would disguise her nerves. Who was Mr Shepard? And how did the woman know her name? She guessed her dad or Bill must have mentioned it. 'Shall I leave my things here?' She pointed down at her bucket.

'No, bring them, too. We don't want anyone tripping over them and suing us.' The woman gave a mirthless laugh.

Millie wished she *could* leave her bucket so her dad might wonder where she was. Although since he'd disappeared ten minutes ago himself, maybe that wouldn't help. Millie waved to the security man and called, 'See you in a minute,' as she walked off towards the staircase. He mimed a question at her and she gave a big pantomime shrug back. No, she had no idea where she was being taken, either.

Chapter Thirteen

Elaine took Millie up two flights of stairs, down a corridor, turned right, and then down another corridor. Millie thought she must now be at the back of the building, but she found her sense of direction impaired by the fact that all the corridors looked the same. They came to a door on the right and the woman knocked briskly.

'Come in,' called a voice.

She opened the door into a smart, functional office. There was a large wooden desk in the middle of the room, and behind that sat a pasty-looking man who might have been about the same age as Millie's dad. It was hard to tell. He was the kind of person you forgot about the second after you laid eyes upon him. He was average height, average weight, had mousy hair and eyebrows, boring glasses, a grey suit, a navy tie and no distinguishing features whatsoever. Behind him was a row of filing cabinets, and on his desk was a grey computer that could have done with a good dusting.

Apparently, in the absence of the cleaners, absolutely nothing got cleaned.

'This is Millie,' said Elaine.

'Hello, Millie,' said the forgettable man, in his forgettable voice. 'My name's Arthur Shepard.'

'Hello.' Millie stared back at him, trying to absorb what she could about him and his office without seeming too interested. 'Did you want your windows cleaned?'

'Ah, no, perhaps not today.'

'Oh,' said Millie, as Elaine left the room, closing the door softly behind her.

'I wondered if I could ask you a few questions,' said Arthur Shepard.

Millie was entirely familiar with this grammatical construction, as she had had a particularly poisonous woman teaching her physics the year before who had phrased her sentences in exactly the same way: it sounded like a friendly question or a polite request, but it was always, definitely, an order. There was never the option to reply, for example, 'How interesting for you. Well, keep wondering,' and wander off happily with no further information about sound waves, for example, clogging up your brain.

'Sure,' Millie said. 'About windows?' This was the technique she had generally employed with the toxic Mrs Greenaway. Helpful, but stupid, so she had nothing to work with.

'No, no.' He smiled insincerely. 'Not about windows.'

'Oh.' Millie stared again. Hopefully, he would soon decide she was too dense to have helped a cat escape from a pet shop, let alone a secure testing laboratory.

'You were here on Tuesday, were you not?'

'What day is it now?' Millie decided that if she were going to play dumb, she might as well enjoy it.

'Thursday.'

'Is it?'

'Yes.'

Millie was pleased to note that he sounded a bit tetchy now – he didn't have Mrs Greenaway's legendary patience, then.

'Er, I think so, then, yes. Yes,' she said.

'You were cleaning the doors downstairs, I think?'

'Oh, you want to talk about doors. Not windows.'

'Not entirely, no. Just the doors downstairs, that lead to the outside of the building.'

'Right. Yes, then.'

'Yes what?'

'Yes, I was cleaning those doors.' Millie could see that the man was getting very tired of her unhelpful helpfulness. Good.

'Excellent. That's what I thought. Now, while you were cleaning the doors, at around five past three, did you see anything?'

'I don't know.'

'What do you mean, you don't know?' The man now sounded exactly like Mrs Greenaway when someone explained that they didn't know quite how light travelled across the vacuum of space, but that bicycles might be involved.

'I don't know what time it is, ever. My watch is broken.' Millie hadn't quite got round to telling her dad that she'd drowned it, and was therefore still wearing it to fend off awkward questions. She held it out for the man to see, so he could verify her story. He didn't even glance at it. She carried on: 'It's not waterproof, you see, and I put my arm in the bucket, and so it . . .' She trailed off, as even the stupidest person could see he wasn't listening.

'Did you see anything at any time at all?' His forgettable voice had now taken on a distinct tone of irritation.

'I saw the security man on the desk through the doors. He's nice.'

'Apart from him.'

'I saw my dad and Bill up on the platform. I never get to go on that.'

Mr Shepard looked torn between telling her this was a good idea – as she was obviously too young and stupid to be allowed near anything dangerous, starting with cutlery and ending with window cleaners' cradles – and telling her she should immediately be hoisted three floors up, surrounded by kitchen knives, blindfolded, and forced to fend for herself.

'And I saw the man in the white coat.'

Arthur Shepard bit back the obvious reply.

'Which man?' he asked, in what he imagined was a patient voice.

'The one looking for . . .' Millie trailed off. She couldn't remember exactly what the man had said. Had he mentioned a cat? She didn't think so.

'The one looking for . . . somebody. He seemed pretty upset. Did he find him?'

'No, he didn't. We're still trying to help him do that now. Did *you* see anything?'

'No. He asked me that before. Did you ask my dad? They were higher up, they might have seen someone. Oh, they were probably looking at the windows, though. It's the best way to get them clean, I think.' Millie's heart was racing. Should she have said 'something', not 'someone'? Maybe not – she was supposed to think it was a person who was missing, wasn't she? He'd asked her if she'd seen 'anything', though, and not 'anyone'. Maybe he wouldn't notice. This was the trouble with lying, it was so hard to think how you would behave if you were telling the truth.

'Yes, I fear they were. Well, thank you for your time, young lady.' Millie tried to remain calm, as there was still time to make a mistake. 'You can get back to your work now.'

'OK.' Millie stood up and turned round. There was a filing cabinet behind the door which she hadn't been able to see as she came in. On top of the filing cabinet was a bendy plastic robot which Millie knew was expensive, because her friend Claire's little brother, Joe, had wanted one last Christmas. The toy was of some kind of special plastic that meant it moved like a toy robot, and came with a remote control, but it was also stretchy and flexible, like Plasticine, if you held it in your hands to warm it up a bit. Claire's mum and dad had tried to get him one, but everywhere had sold out by mid-November, and he had been pretty disappointed on Christmas Day. Then it turned out that none of his friends had got one either, and he minded a bit less. The toys were still in extremely short supply, and Joe was now hoping to get one for his birthday, or even next Christmas.

'Thank you,' said Arthur Shepard firmly, opening the door for her.

Mille smiled gormlessly as the woman reappeared to take her back downstairs. But she was curious: in an office otherwise devoid of personal things – no pictures, no photographs, no funny cartoons pinned to the wall – why would a man like Arthur Shepard have a children's toy sitting on his filing cabinet?

'Now, how old are you?' asked Elaine, as she walked Millie back down the corridor.

'Twelve,' she replied.

'Goodness, are you?' the woman said, betraying not even the slightest hint of interest in her voice. 'I hope we won't get in trouble with Personnel for having an under-sixteen working here.'

'I'm just helping my dad,' said Millie. This woman was beginning to annoy her.

'Well, so long as you're not on the payroll, I suppose what they don't know won't hurt them. Now, do you think you could carry some bags of rubbish down to the rubbish room? The cleaners aren't in today. They're not heavy. They're all paper, really.' Millie restrained herself from asking if the cleaners were really made of paper, and from pointing out that paper can be extremely heavy if you have enough of it, and nodded. Maybe this was her chance to get a look at some of the scientists' work. Riffling through bins wasn't terribly glamorous, but needs must. They had now reached the stairwell which she had come up earlier, and she turned as if to go back down. The woman reached out and stopped her.

'Good,' she said, and pointed up to the third floor. 'I've had the staff put the bags at the top of the stairs – just up there. I think they're technically a fire hazard until you've moved them, so the sooner the better, really. The rubbish room is at the bottom of these stairs – ground floor, first door on the left. Just dump them all in there.'

'OK,' said Millie.

The woman turned around and stalked back towards Arthur Shepard's office. Millie ran up the stairs – finally, this was her chance to see what was going on. There must have been twenty black bin liners full of rubbish. She was just about to open one of the bags when a tiny noise caught her attention. She followed the sound and saw the little CCTV camera winking at her across the stairwell. She couldn't assume that she would be lucky twice. She sighed and picked up the rubbish bag, and began to carry it downstairs. The woman might have been rude, but she had also been right – it wasn't heavy at all. She manoeuvred open the doors downstairs, banging one elbow painfully as she went, and put the bag in a large empty room, with bolted doors that presumably led outside for the rubbish to be picked up by lorry. She looked around quickly. There were no cameras in here. This was her chance. She carefully, carefully untied the top, so she could retie it when she was finished and leave it looking just the same. She opened it, looked inside, and gasped in disappointment. No wonder the bag was light. The small amount of paper inside had been shredded into tiny pieces – there was no hope of reading even a single word. She bit her lip in annoyance, retied the bag, and went back upstairs. Surely one of them would have something in that wasn't less than half an inch square? Or maybe someone used a very small font, so she could at least find out something off one fragment.

Seventeen bags later, she realised that the scientists were obviously more thorough than she had thought. Each bag had been filled with shreds and nothing else. Millie felt like crying, she was so frustrated. Here was possibly all the information she could wish for, handed to her like a Christmas present, only one that was missing its batteries, and had additionally been stamped on by a weighty and malevolent sibling. She had four more bags to go, but she was still going to check them all, just in case.

When she went back up to get the next one, she found that the bags had been hiding a door. Maybe she could sneak through it and explore the third floor – this was where Max had been kept, after all. Millie felt her heart begin to pound for maybe the fifth time that day. She leaned gently on the door, and it moved slightly. She leaned a little harder, and it opened a few inches.

She was just about to try and look round, when a voice said, 'Hello? Can I help you?' A man opened the door slightly further and peered round the side of it. He was wearing a white lab coat and holding onto the door suspiciously, like a dressing-gowned homeowner with his door on a security chain.

'Sorry,' said Millie, thinking that at least after today she knew her heart contained no defects or weaknesses, because if it had, she would have died several times over. 'I fell into the door,' she said, rubbing her elbow to give some conviction to the story. Luckily, she had smacked it so many times on the doors downstairs, it was already quite red.

'Easily done,' said the man. 'Take more care of yourself, won't you?' He shut the door firmly in her face, and she picked up another bag and carried it grimly back downstairs.

She opened it with no expectation of finding anything more than she had in the others, but this one was slightly different. On top of the shredded paper were several sheets of newspaper, folded over. Millie sniffed – she could definitely smell something that wasn't newsprint, and she thought it was almost certainly cat. Maybe they used newspaper to line the cages. She would ask Max. She looked through the pages and realised it was a paper from last week, almost complete, though it appeared to be missing the middle sheet. She sighed, returned the newspaper to the bag and retied it. The last few bags were soon done and checked, all containing exactly the same shreds as the rest. Millie had only one more idea, and that was to leave the outer doors unbolted, so that maybe she and Max and the protesters would be able to get through one evening, and try to free the other cats. She unhooked the bolts and left the doors shut, putting a couple of bags in front of them, so you couldn't see the bolts. Almost immediately, the inner door opened and Elaine walked in.

'All done?' she asked and, without waiting for a reply, went on: 'Good. Now, if you could just unbolt those doors, so the men can pick this lot up in the morning . . .'

Millie stared. They left the doors open overnight? She would have no problem coming to rescue Max's friends – they were practically being *invited* in. She went to the doors and tried to look like she was undoing the bolts.

'Thanks,' said the woman, and held the inner door open for her to go back to the lobby. Millie walked past her, then watched as the woman produced two enormous keys and locked the inside door from the corridor side. Stupid – of course they didn't leave the building open overnight. Mille sighed inwardly one more time. Breaking the rest of the cats out wasn't going to be quite as easy as she'd hoped.

Chapter Fourteen

Millie arrived back home dying to tell Max about everything that had happened. She was sure that Arthur Shepard was the one behind the cat-napping. No, that didn't sound quite right. Kit-napping. That would do. She'd asked her dad and Bill where they'd gone off to, and they both muttered something about cleaning the upper floors. Millie wanted to ask them what they'd seen up there, but realised her dad wasn't going to say anything very much, in case she got upset about testing animals again. Too late, Millie thought grimly – I've got one of their animals already. She went to the back door and opened it for Max, pretending she wanted to let some fresh air into the house. She expected to see him come darting in immediately, but there was no sign of him. She wandered around the kitchen for a while, making a drink, finding a biscuit, looking out of the window. Still nothing. Weird. Her dad came in to boil the kettle, and the opportunity was lost. She went up to her room and shut the door behind her, feeling at a loose end.

'Psst,' said a voice from under the bed.

'Max?'

'Of course Max. Who else would be hiding under your bed? Is this a comic opera?' The sleek blue-grey cat sidled his way out from beneath the bed with a grace that was only slightly marred by the large balls of dust behind his ears.

'I don't know,' said Millie. 'What's a comic opera? Is it drawings of fat people?'

Max rolled his eyes. 'You have no culture at all,' he replied.

'Never mind that. How did you get in? I've got so much to tell you.'

'And I have a lot to tell you. You want to know how I got in? I got in when the people who came to search your house opened the window.'

'*What?* You're joking.' Millie gaped at him.

'I'm quite serious. Two men arrived after you had gone.'

'How long after?' she asked.

'I meant to check my watch, but then I remembered. I can't find one that looks right against my fur.'

'Thank you.' Millie rolled her eyes back at him.

'Before lunchtime, definitely.'

'How did they get in? Did they have a key?'

'I don't know. I was in the back garden. I didn't see them get in, I just saw them when they went into the kitchen. The side-window of your garage is open, though, and the brick-work beneath it looks scuffed, so I think they got in there. I watched them going up the stairs, so I jumped onto the garage roof, and then I waited outside the bathroom window. I knew they would open a window upstairs, because it's been so hot today. When they left the bathroom one open, I jumped in.'

'Are you mental? What if they'd seen you?' Millie cried.

'I am not, as you say, mental,' Max said stiffly. 'I am silent and cunning. I heard them talking in your father's room, I knew the coast was clear, I jumped in and I hid. This is what cats are good at. One of the *many* things we are good at,' he corrected himself.

'But the risk was huge.' Millie was still appalled. 'What did they do next?'

'They searched your dad's room for a while, and the other bedroom. Then they tried yours. They checked for cat hair on the bed – it's lucky I am too polite to moult. Also, I think they were put off by all the dust. One of them kept sneezing.'

'That's lucky. I knew it would come in handy sooner or later – I keep telling Dad that housework is dangerous. What did they do then?'

'Then they turned on your computer.'

'How did that go?'

'Badly for them.'

'Great.'

'They accessed your email account.'

'My regular one?'

'Does it have two messages in, one from your grandparents

in Australia and one from your friend Claire who is in Italy on holiday?'

'That's the one.'

'Yes, they checked that. They seemed a little disappointed that you didn't have more mail.'

'I'm a surprisingly efficient correspondent.'

'That's good.'

'Did they check the Deleted Items?'

'Apparently you have none. Just a few emails from somewhere, asking you if you'd like a special-offer DVD, whatever that might be.'

'I empty it pretty often. I leave those ones in so it doesn't look suspiciously empty.'

'Suspicious to whom? Have you lived your whole life expecting something like this to happen? You are extraordinary.'

'I told you – my dad is nuts about computer privacy. That's why I have a Mac – they're harder to attack with viruses.'

'The computer can become ill?'

'Yeah, kind of. And people can send you stuff which can get them information about your machine. They're called Worms. Or Trojans.'

'Oh.' Max looked confused.

'Anyway, my dad thinks that if you only store the things you can't keep in your head on the computer, there's less for someone to steal, so I delete everything I can, and keep my vital stuff on a memory stick, which I carry ar—'

'Please don't take this the wrong way. I'm impressed, and yet simultaneously not interested.'

'It's fine. I slightly wish I'd rescued another cat.'

'I slightly wish you had, too.' Max looked huffy.

Millie laughed.

'Ah, I *am* interested in one thing,' said Max.

'What's that?'

'Your father is a computer expert, yet he is cleaning windows for a job. Why is that?'

'Oh, well . . .' Millie looked embarrassed, as though she were giving away her dad's secrets. 'He lost his job about three months ago. And I thought he'd be applying for other jobs, but he doesn't seem to want to. Or maybe he does want to, but his friend thinks he's lost his belief in himself. Only, we don't have very much spare money, because there's only my dad and me. My mum died years ago, and my grandparents are in Australia, and they don't even know he's lost his job, so . . .' She trailed off.

'That is nothing to be ashamed of,' Max said. 'He is earning money the best way he can, until the right thing comes along. I think that's very dignified. Very fatherly.'

'Me too, I guess.' Millie smiled. 'Anyway, what happened next? I mean, today?'

'Nothing,' he replied. 'They tried to check your internet history, but that didn't seem to work at all.'

'Yup. That's what's supposed to happen. Then what did they do?'

'They gave up. They thought it had been a waste of time from the beginning. They put everything back where it was, and let themselves out of the front door.'

'Interesting. Let me tell you what was happening to us at the same time.'

Millie told him everything, and watched the disappointment flit across his face, mirroring her own, when she explained about the locked doors, the too-attentive third-floor staff, and the endless frustration of the fruitless rubbish search. He confirmed that the cats did indeed sit on newspaper, and made acerbic comments about the taste in reading matter of two of the lab techs. He listened carefully as she told him the part about Arthur Shepard. But Max didn't recognise him from her description – he had no idea who had captured him, because he'd never seen the man's face. And inside the laboratory, he had only seen the scientists and technicians.

'I'm sure he's the one in charge of this thing,' Millie finished. 'Let's look him up and see what we find out.'

She googled Arthur Shepard, and tracked down his work history right up to his current employment at Vakkson. There wasn't a huge amount of information. 'I'll try the library tomorrow,' she decided. 'I can probably find out where he lives and stuff from there.'

'You are a little frightening sometimes,' said Max.

'He started it.'

'That's true.'

'I'll check the mailbox, too – see if the protesters have got back to us.'

Millie found a new mail from the *.co.uk* protester, whom she'd decided she liked less than the other one, and clicked on it. It was just one line:

> can find out nothing about a project using cats
> there. will look into it. do nothing till you hear
> from us again.

'That's pretty firm,' said Max.

'Mmm,' said Millie. 'Do you get the feeling they're freezing us out?'

'I don't understand what you mean,' said the cat, sighing. They hadn't really got their metaphors sorted yet.

'I mean, we're not supposed to do anything till they find out more. They've had two days to find stuff out, and they haven't. Look what we've been doing in that time. They just stand outside the laboratory each day and shout. What more are they going to find out, doing that?'

'You think there is something . . .' Max cast around for the phrase, not to be outdone, 'something, ah, *fishy*, going on?'

'Yes,' said Millie, trying and failing to suppress a grin. 'That *is* what I think. Well, maybe not fishy, exactly – they might not be suspicious, but they're certainly no help.'

'What should we do, then?' he asked.

'Ask the other ones to help us?' she suggested.

'The "direct action" ones? You don't think they might be a little crazy?'

'Maybe. Do you think helping a twelve-year-old girl and a talking cat to break into a secure laboratory to rescue some other talking cats is a job that any sane people would be likely to agree to?'

Max shrugged. 'That's a fair point.'

Millie typed back to the fishy protesters:

> whatever you say. we'll wait till we hear from you.

'And you have such an innocent face,' said Max, shaking his head.

'Let's hope they fall for it,' she muttered, hoping rather than believing that this would be the case. Then she mailed the crazy ones:

> crates of cats were brought in two weeks ago, at the back of the lab, away from the road. they know you're watching – they're avoiding you deliberately. we're planning a break-out. will you help us?

She pressed 'Send'.

'How can they help us?' Max asked.

'I hope they can help us carry out the rescue mission. We can't do it on our own. There's at least one security guard with at least one Alsatian patrolling the building perimeter. The security guy told me that. The CCTV cameras are on and recording at night – they're inside and outside the building. We definitely can't get the cats out during the day – there are too many people there. Actually, that's a good question.'

'What is?'

'How did *you* get out during the day?'

'I was cunning,' Max began grandly.

'I never doubted it. That lab tech looked like an idiot, though.'

'Well, that certainly helped.' Max acknowledged the helping hand of stupidity in his grand plan. 'I had been planning it since the day I arrived. I had been chewing at the catch on my cage every time no one could see me. It was quite loose to begin with, because the room is sealed, and the cage doors have to be easy to open and shut with one hand while you hold an annoyed cat in the other one.'

'How is the room sealed?'

Max thought for a second. 'There are two doors. The second one will not open while the first one is open.'

'Like an airlock?' Millie asked.

Max looked quizzical.

'In a submarine?' she suggested.

'Yes, exactly like that. I am a world-renowned expert on submarines, of course.'

'You've seen a James Bond film,' Millie said. 'They all have submarines in.'

'Really?'

'Most of them do. The ones that don't have spaceships in. Spaceships with airlocks.'

'Well, I must have failed to pay attention,' said Max serenely. 'Anyway, you appear to have the idea. So I escaped from the cage, which was easy, because, as you noticed, that man was not very good at his job. I hid behind him, and snuck through the door as he did. The second door opened, and then a noise sounded, like an alarm. So I ran straight past him and down the stairs: the stair door was propped open with a fire extinguisher.'

'Simple, but brilliant,' Millie congratulated him.

Max shrugged modestly. 'I thought so.'

'So,' Millie pondered, as she would a tricky equation, 'the alarm only sounded when the second door opened. Had you heard it go off before?'

'No, never. The lab techs used to come in and out all the time, and it never went off. To be honest, when it did go off, I was pretty . . .' He looked pained. 'Is the word I want here "alarmed"?'

Millie laughed. 'Yes,' she said. 'Is that your first pun?'

'And my last. I guarantee it.'

'Did the lab techs come in one at a time, or together?'

Max tried to think. 'One by one. I am sure of it.'

'Then I think there must be a motion sensor there that picks up two people in the lock, well, one person, one cat, instead of just the usual one. And it's on the outer door, so that suggests they're more worried about people coming *in* than cats going *out*. That's useful to know. And the door to the stairs would normally be shut, because they all have signs on – at least all the ones I saw do – saying they're fire doors, and they have to be kept shut. So someone must have just propped it open to get some air. It was hot that day, wasn't it?'

'The windows don't open on the top floor. There was no fresh air in there.'

'That makes sense, then. You were pretty lucky.'

'And very skilled,' Max reminded her.

'That too. This is all stuff we need to think about for the rescue. I think it has to be at night – we couldn't get that lucky again. And so much for leaving a window open and hoping for the best. I was really hoping we could get in through the rubbish room, where I spent most of this afternoon. But it's no good – I saw that woman lock it from the inside. We can't do it on our own,' she declared. 'We'll need those protesters to help us.'

'Will they?'

'I don't know. We'll have to wait and see. They raid laboratories sometimes – I've seen it on the news. We just need to persuade them to do Haverham,' she said thoughtfully.

'And soon,' Max reminded her. 'Monty and Celeste, they are waiting for me.'

'Yes, soon. I think we're going to have to pretend to be disgruntled former employees with insider information.'

'That is virtually the truth, apart from the bit where you

only worked outside the building, and I was there against my will, and not getting paid.'

'OK, I'm going to think about it tonight. You go outside in case those men come back. We'll reconvene tomorrow morning,' Millie said decisively.

'Reconvene?' Max looked perplexed.

'Meet again.'

'Why do you not say that?'

'I dunno. "Reconvene" sounds better. More military.' She looked slightly embarrassed.

'You want to sound like a soldier?' asked the cat.

Millie looked him squarely in his luminous eyes. 'Isn't this a fight?'

'Of course.' Max skimmed past Millie's arm as she reached up to open the window for him. 'I'm glad it was you I ran into,' he whispered, rubbing his head on her wrist.

'Me too. I mean, I don't really wish you'd been another cat,' she replied, and she ran her fingers through the velvet fur between his ears.

'Are you sure you don't want me to bring you a nice dead bird, as a gift?' he asked in a kindly voice.

'Scram, pesky cat.' She rolled her eyes at him, laughing again. 'See you tomorrow.' But he had already disappeared, eaten alive by the shadows around him. It wasn't cold, but still Millie shivered, and shut the window fast, hugging her arms around her.

Chapter Fifteen

Millie spent the night watching TV with her dad, only half-concentrating on the programmes, and thinking hard. She went to bed and slept badly, jumping awake as she dreamed of Arthur Shepard in her house, going through her things and combing her computer for secrets. She wished Max had spent the night indoors, and as she fell back to sleep, she dreamed that he had been caught again, stuffed back in a box and taken away.

She was very glad when it was morning, although she felt as tired as she had been when she went to bed. She looked suspiciously at the computer, still seeing Arthur Shepard's nightmare fingers on its keyboard. She opened it, and the screen flashed up exactly as she had left it, the clock showing the time she had last used it for just a second before it woke up properly and remembered which day it was. Millie tried to shake the bad dreams from her head – look, here was proof that the computer hadn't been touched, and that no one had been near it but her. Still, she went online to check her mail with a twitchy feeling in her stomach. At least, she thought that's what it was, but it could just have been a really fervent desire for toast.

There was only one message this time, from the direct-action protesters:

wednesday? 11pm?

Millie finally heeded the call to toast, and went downstairs.

Her dad had gone out early, and left a big note on the kitchen table telling her to eat something sensible and that he'd be back around four. Millie went to the front door and pulled the security chain across. Then she went to check the window locks and fastened each one. She wasn't taking any chances if those men had been able to get in yesterday.

She found Max at the French windows and let him in before bolting those shut, too.

'Are you all right?' asked the cat, noticing the circles beneath her eyes.

'Slept badly,' she explained. 'I need to get on with this plan, because I won't sleep well until I do.'

'You *should* be worried,' Max said. 'I am, too.'

'Great,' Millie sighed. 'OK, here's what I think we should do. We've got to aim to get into the laboratory on Wednesday. The protesters can help us then – I checked our mail first thing this morning. We'll need an excuse so Dad doesn't notice we're missing. I don't know how we pull that one off. I might have to arrange to go to a friend's, someone who's on holiday or something. We'll bike out to the lab – it's only about three miles away, if we go cross-country – which will be dark, so that might be a bit dangerous, but we're less likely to be seen, which is good. We'll meet the protesters at eleven o'clock – at least, that's what they said in their email. That should be late enough for all the staff to have gone, and it will have been dark for a couple of hours. Now, presuming they agree, we go to the building with some of them, while the rest keep an eye out for the guard and the dog.' Max bristled. 'Or guards and dogs,' she continued. 'I don't know how many there are. We need the protesters to help us cut the power to the building – that's the big problem.'

'Why do we need to do that?'

'Otherwise, the alarms will go off and the cameras will record us. So, then we race upstairs, and go into the lab—'

'Wait,' interrupted Max. 'How?'

'How what?'

'How do we get into the lab if the electricity is off? The doors are automatic.'

Millie looked at him, horrified.

'Of course.' She slumped down in her chair, crushed. 'I don't know. I don't know what to do. If the electricity stays on, the alarms will pick us up. And so will the cameras. And if the power is cut, the doors won't open. Could we break them open?' she asked hopefully. 'I don't suppose they're made of thin glass or anything?'

'No, they are metal, with a thick round window in the top half of each one.'

'OK.' They sat in silence for several minutes, Millie biting her lip furiously.

'Would it have helped if I'd said they were made of paper? Thin tissue paper?' asked Max.

'Are they?'

'No.'

'Then no,' she said sadly. 'It wouldn't have helped. I mean, the planning would have been easier, but the plan itself probably wouldn't have been much good.'

'Stop,' said Max softly. 'You shouldn't be sad. We have done amazing things. You have rescued me and kept me safe. You have seen the inside of that man's office. You have made a plan, which is very good and just needs a little refining.'

'It's not good. It's rubbish,' Millie wailed. 'How can we open the doors and not set off the alarms? We don't stand a chance.'

'We will mail our co-conspirators. Perhaps they can help.'

Millie looked cheered at the prospect of something concrete to do. She ran upstairs with Max close on her tail, and clicked on her inbox. She replied to the protesters' earlier email.

next wed, 11pm is fine. problem – how can we cut the power to switch off the alarms and cameras, when the cats are behind an electronic door?

She sent the message, and they sat and gazed at the screen.

'This is silly,' Millie said suddenly. 'They won't mail if we're sitting here watching. They probably have jobs, after all, and can only email sometimes. Let's go and do something else. We'll check every hour.' The two of them went back downstairs and Max lay under the windows, basking in the sun, while Millie tried to concentrate on a book. She made lunch, and Max played with some cat food, obviously wishing it would put up more of a fight. They watched a film, and tried to distract themselves from watching the clock.

On the fourth check, there was a reply.

name the meeting place. don't worry about the electricity – it's sorted.

'What?' Millie exploded. She typed back:

what do you mean, 'it's sorted'?

This time, they replied immediately:

don't worry. the power will do what it's told next week.

'What does *that* mean?' asked Max, rubbing his head fondly on Millie's arm, like a normal cat. He had been worried by her today – she seemed like such a calm, sensible girl: she hadn't shrieked when he first spoke to her, she hadn't gone crazy when the house had been searched, she hadn't ever seemed even slightly upset about any of this, only annoyed that he should have been taken from his home, and determined to help him. Then suddenly the thought of not being able to break and enter into a secure facility at his request had left her frustrated, even panicky. He was touched.

Millie read the second sentence out loud, paused for a moment as she thought about it, and said, 'I have absolutely no idea.'

Chapter Sixteen

The week dragged by endlessly. Millie tried to kill time at the library, looking for more information about Arthur Shepard than she had been able to discover online, but she had no luck. His address seemed to be unregistered everywhere. She was bored and nervous at the same time, which was making her twitchier than ever – she couldn't remember how it felt not to wake up in a cold sweat after a horrible dream had left her sickened. She wished there was more they could do, but she and Max had been over the map of the building and the plan for the break-in a dozen times. She demolished all the books she had borrowed and headed off to the library to keep herself busy while Max was out eating hapless woodland creatures.

As she was replacing her books and retrieving new ones, her eye was caught by the new signs on the wall, one of which told her where the microfilm section was. She had never been to that part of the library and wandered in for a look around. There was nobody there at all – it seemed that the newspaper archives were not a particular draw in Haverham. She scanned the shelves, and had a thought – why had the newspaper which she had found in the rubbish been missing its middle pages? What had been on it that one of the lab technicians had wanted to keep? Probably a crossword puzzle, she thought irritably. No – that couldn't be it, because those were on the back page. She tracked down the microfilm of the correct date and paper, and searched through it. She found the missing part, which was a double sheet from the middle – four pages of news. Well, three pages of news, because the first page was a huge picture of a supermodel wearing virtually nothing. Millie looked around hastily. She hoped nobody thought she was weird, looking at pictures of naked women, and she flicked quickly to the next page. The other three pages were boring business news – software and telecom share prices up, clothing retail and toy manufacturer share prices down. Millie wasn't entirely sure how shares worked, but she couldn't believe that the lab techs had cared much more than she did. They must have wanted the picture of the girl. She put the microfilm away, annoyed.

'It was a good idea, though,' Max consoled her, when she grumbled about it later.

'*I* thought so,' she sighed, thinking of her fruitless search through all those bags of rubbish, her attempts to get onto the third floor of the laboratory, her hopes of getting in through the rubbish room, and now this. She hoped her ideas would start working out soon. The next day, in fact, when they would put stage one of their plan into action.

Millie told her dad that she would be staying at Sarah's on Wednesday.

'I'll need to speak to her parents,' was all he said.

'Sure,' she replied anxiously. 'I'll get them to ring you.'

She thought for a while. When Max appeared from the garden, she said, 'How good a liar are you?'

'The best, of course. Why?' Max's face fell, as he realised suddenly that he might just have talked himself into trouble.

'I have an idea . . .' Millie said.

'Just going to the library, Dad,' she called out as she swung her leg over her old bicycle and shoved her bag in the basket.

'Ow,' muttered the bag.

'Sorry,' she whispered.

She rode to the woods which were on the way to the laboratory. They were unfenced, and it would, as far as she could see, be easy to get through them, even in the dark, although she would definitely need a torch. And spare batteries. She added these to her mental list. She pedalled away to a nearby field, propped her bike up against the fence, and looked around to check that they couldn't be overheard by passing dog-walkers or farmers.

'OK, coast's clear,' she said, and opened the bag.

Max jumped free and looked around.

'Didn't you think we should be somewhere a bit more hidden?' He was rather grumpy after the long, dark, uncomfortable journey.

'Nope. If they can't see us, we might not be able to see them. Here, we can see a mile or more in every direction. No one's going to sneak up on us.'

Max thought again what an excellent spy Millie would make.

'Ready?' she asked.

He cleared his throat dramatically.

'Ready. What's the name again?'

'My dad's? Alan,' she said.

'Not *his* name, *my* name,' said the cat patiently.

'Oh, yeah. Derek.' Millie smacked her fist onto her forehead – this lack of sleep was making her a bit dense. She pulled her phone out of her pocket, dialled 141, and then her home number. It rang out twice, three times, and then her dad picked up.

'Hello?' She held it quickly to Max's ear.

'Hello?' said Max. 'Is that Alan Raven?'

'Speaking,' said her dad.

'This is Derek, Sarah's dad,' continued Max.

'Oh, hello.'

'I was calling to see if Millie can come over on Wednesday night.'

'Sure, of course she can. I just wanted to talk to you to check it was OK,' said Alan.

'We're looking forward to having her,' said Max, pulling a face at Millie to say this acting natural thing was not coming easily. Millie smirked back.

'Well, we'd love to have Sarah round some time, too.' Millie's dad was polite to a fault.

'She'd love that. Ah, is that the doorbell?'

Millie began shaking with silent laughter, her nervousness about this stage of the plan making her giggly.

'Excuse me,' Max said, with as much dignity as he could muster, 'I'm afraid there's someone at my door.'

'Oh, sure,' said Millie's dad. 'Well, nice to talk to you. Bye.'

'Bye,' said Max, and Millie pressed the 'End Call' button before collapsing into laughter.

'Was that the best you could come up with? "There's someone at the door"?' She was prostrate on the ground.

'It was difficult,' Max said, now sounding injured. 'I don't like lying to your dad – I like him.'

'You haven't even met him.'

'I've *heard* him. That's the same thing.'

'OK, international super spy, it's the same thing.'

'There's no need to be quite so rude.'

'Sorry.' Millie was chastened by his hurt face. 'I'm not really laughing because it's funny. I think I'm slightly hysterical because that's the first part of our plan in place.'

'It is, isn't it?' said Max.

Millie nodded. Max rubbed his head hard against her leg. She scritched his ears. They had begun.

On the other side of the wood, Arthur Shepard sat at his desk, wondering. He had spoken to the window cleaner, his colleague, and his daughter, and all had professed to know nothing. He didn't know which man had been lying to him, but he was sure one of them had. It obviously wasn't the girl – Mickey and Ray had checked her bedroom and her computer out the day before, and she was just a child. But someone had been trying to get information from the protesters – *his* protesters. The messages had come through to him, of course, and he had approved the reply, telling whichever thieving crook it was who had seen his cat, maybe even stolen his cat, to sit tight and wait for further information. Which would come in a few weeks, when everything was finished. Still, whoever it was had been looking him up on the internet – he had set up an expensive alarm system some months ago, which alerted him when anyone tried to find out anything about him through electoral registers and the like. And the alarm had been triggered the previous day. He tracked down the service provider and the telephone number and cursed with rage when it led him only to the local library. It must have been one of the window cleaners – no one else could know anything, he had been too careful. But whoever it was was being cautious, covering their tracks. And yet, there had been no demand for money, no tabloids ringing up with their exposé, nothing. He couldn't work it out. If one of them knew what was going on – worse, if one of them had the damned cat as evidence – why weren't they selling what they knew, either to him or to the press?

He had spent twenty-four hours weighing up the pros and cons of his decision, and he had come to a conclusion. The cats would be transferred to another lab, as soon as possible. Next week at the latest. He would need to make some calls.

Chapter Seventeen

Millie and Max were already fidgeting with nerves by Wednesday morning. Millie had woken up every hour of every night, and grey circles smudged under her eyes. Max liked to think he was hiding it a little better, but he too looked nervous and edgy. They had arranged to meet the protesters at eleven o'clock that evening. At first, Millie had been worried that it would be too early, and maybe the security guards would be less enthusiastic later in the night. But her dad thought she was going over to Sarah's at eight, and now the day had finally arrived, Millie realised that by the time they had biked over there, they would still have to wait for about two hours in the woods, which was more than long enough.

She packed her bag carefully, taking a navy jumper with a hood, the map they had drawn of the building, a torch and spare batteries, a fully charged phone she had already set to silent, so there would be no nasty shocks if it suddenly started ringing, her bike lights, because it would be dark when they came home, and chocolate, in case either of them needed a sugar rush later on. She wore dark jeans, black trainers, and a navy T-shirt, and hoped that in the dark she would be pretty hard to see.

Max wore his usual dark grey fur, and looked on smugly at Millie's complex preparations. They left the house at eight o'clock, and by half past eight they were on the edge of the woods. Millie picked an unusually large oak tree and hid her bike underneath it. There were plenty of dead leaves and bracken, and soon she had concealed the bike from view. She made a large scratch in the tree at eye-level, feeling guilty as she scarred the huge trunk and subverted everything her dad had told her about environmental responsibility. But she couldn't afford to lose time later trying to remember which tree it had been, and it was mostly moss that she had removed. She and Max sat and talked, distracting each other in whispers, about Ixelles, Max's home, and his family – smart, practical Sofie, whom he had picked when she came to a cat breeder's several years before, with her son, Stef. Stef was now thirteen, and Max had largely forgiven, if not entirely forgotten, his early tail-pulling years. Sofie was a kind woman who had patiently helped Stef with his English and Dutch homework, little realising that Max was picking up trilingual skills as well.

Stef would like Millie, Max thought, and she him – although he was quite a dreamy boy, which Millie might find a bit irritating at first. She would get over it, though. He hoped he would have the chance to introduce them.

It was quarter to ten. They padded silently through the woods, following the compass set into the bottom of Millie's torch, but keeping the light off – the plan was to use it only after the escape, when speed was absolutely necessary. Max could see easily in the dark, and could guide Millie around trees that suddenly leapt out of total blackness, or troughs that would suddenly fall away beneath her feet. They had arranged to meet the protesters on the far side of the wood, about fifty feet inside it, where the security men shouldn't be able to see them. They were a few minutes early, and they waited behind a tree for the sound of more people arriving. At five to eleven, Millie was getting worried.

'What if they're not coming?' she hissed.

'I don't know. It's still early. They will come.' Max tried to sound more confident than he felt, which was not at all. They waited a few more minutes. At two minutes past the hour, Millie began to despair.

'We'll have to go home. We can't do it on our own. They aren't coming.'

'Shh,' he said. 'I hear something.'

They stood behind their tree, peering round into the darkness.

'I can't hear anything,' she said.

'Shhh. Wait.' And Max was right, Millie heard it too. In just a few moments, their knights in shining armour would appear. The trained, experienced laboratory-breakers, who were going to make everything all right. The noise drew closer. Millie and Max stared.

'Who is that?' whispered Max.

'I don't know,' Millie mumbled back.

'Hello?' said a voice softly. 'Are you there?'

Millie came out from behind the tree to meet the people who were going to divert the guards' attention, control the building's electricity, and generally enable the escape plan to be a success. Or rather, the man. Or, technically, the boy. She was finally face to face with the brains behind the direct-action website, and he appeared to be no more than fifteen years old.

Chapter Eighteen

'Who are you?' she asked quietly.

'I'm Jake. Who are you?'

'I'm Millie.'

'Well, I don't mean to be rude, but I'm supposed to be meeting some people here in secret, and it's quite important, so would you mind leaving?'

'You're meant to be meeting me.' Millie sounded grim.

'What do you mean? I'm here to . . . Oh. That was *you*, emailing?'

'Yep. That was me, emailing.'

'But you're just a little girl.'

'That must get so boring,' Max sympathised. Millie really was very clever and good at things, and yet people patronised her all the time, just because she was young, and looked even younger. He had nearly jumped to the same conclusions himself when he had first met her, and would doubtless have tried to find someone else to rescue him, if there had been anyone else. Luckily for him, there hadn't been.

'Who's that?' said Jake, peering into the darkness.

'My friend, Max,' Millie shot back. 'Where's everyone else?'

'I'm it.'

'What do you mean, you're "it"?' she asked.

'I mean, I'm the one who's coming to help. But this must be some sort of mistake. You can't be planning to break into a secure building. What are you, ten?'

'I'm twelve,' she said through tightly clenched teeth.

'And there are only three of us?' Jake asked, disbelieving.

'I thought you were bringing the other protesters. You said you would.'

'Well, I couldn't. They're not real,' said Jake, looking shifty.

'Of course they're real. I've seen them,' Millie snapped before she realised that wasn't actually true. She had never seen the protesters, nor had Max. They only had her dad's word that they existed at all.

'No, I mean, they are real *people*,' Jake corrected himself. 'Just not real protesters.'

'What do you mean?' asked Max, and Jake looked around, trying to find a face to attach to the voice.

'They're just stooges. Moles, if you like,' Jake said.

Millie heard Max sigh.

'He means that they're just pretending to be protesters,'

she explained, realising that 'mole' wouldn't mean very much to Max, apart from as a concise description of a dinner with poor eyesight and low ground speed. 'Why would anyone do that?' she demanded.

'They're paid by Vakkson to protest outside. They can spy on other people who come and join the protest, and keep Vakkson informed about what's going on. All the animal testers do it now.'

'Oh no,' said Millie. 'We mailed them, too.'

'What did you say?' asked Jake quickly. 'Whatever you told them, they told the people inside the laboratory.'

Millie racked her brains, and recreated the emails she had sent.

'We didn't say anything about a break-out,' she said, hugely relieved.

'Then you're probably all right,' said Jake. 'Anyway, you weren't serious about breaking in, were you?'

'I was and I am,' Millie said simply.

'You're kidding?' Jake was astonished. He assumed she would have reconsidered her plan, now she knew how many co-conspirators she really had.

'Are you going to help or not?' she said testily.

'I thought you said you had insider knowledge. You seemed to know what you were talking about.'

'I do. I've cleaned every window and every door on the ground floor of that building and I know it pretty well. Max has been inside the building, right up in the labs on the top floor, where the cats are. Now – are you in or out?'

Jake stood for a moment, trying to work out how his first attempt at a daring and illegal activity was being dictated by a kid and some bloke he couldn't even see. It was stupid. He should just leave them to it. But he really wanted to go home having achieved something in the real world, not just having sent out salvoes from a computer. Most of all, he really wanted those smug, vicious losers to pay for tormenting harmless creatures. Suddenly, he had an unpleasant thought.

'Hold on. How did Max get into the laboratory, if he's not one of them?'

'He isn't one of them.'

'How can I trust you? You didn't even tell me you were twelve.'

'It didn't come up. Besides, we're trusting *you*,' Millie said sharply.

Jake looked a little abashed. 'You could have said you were just a kid,' he said, trying to regain the moral high ground.

Millie would have none of it. 'So could you. If I prove to you that Max isn't one of them, are you in?'

'Yes.'

'Come on, then.' Millie scooped Max up from the ground and said, 'Jake, meet Max. Max, meet Jake.'

'Hello,' said Max coolly.

Jake jumped backwards.

'How are you doing—?' he asked Millie, eyes wide.

'You think I am some kind of . . .' Max looked at Millie for the word.

'Ventriloquist,' she guessed.

'Thank you,' he said with perfect politeness. Then he turned to Jake and, in a far less polite tone, said, 'You think I am some kind of ventriloquist's dummy?'

Jake looked so shocked that Millie took pity on him.

'Max escaped from the laboratory. This is what they're doing in there – making cats talk. This is why we've got to rescue the rest.'

'Why would they . . .?'

'Do you ever finish sentences?' Max asked irritably. He turned to Millie. 'I have to say, you took it a lot better than this when we met.'

'Why would they want to give voices to cats? We don't know,' Millie said, trying to answer the question she would have asked in Jake's position. 'That's the other thing we need to find out. Now, are you going to keep your side of the bargain?'

'Yes,' Jake breathed. 'So long as that cat stops being mean to me.'

'Max . . .' warned Millie.

'OK,' sighed the cat. 'It was too easy, anyway. It's funnier being mean to you.'

Chapter Nineteen

'So, let's go through the plan again, just to make sure we all know what we're doing,' said Millie, as they pored over the map she had brought. 'Jake, you're going to be the decoy. Get up close to the building, catch the attention of the security blokes, run off, and try not to get caught. If you do get caught, say you're just mucking around, and do a bored teenager thing. OK?'

'OK.' Jake looked way too nervous to be bored, but Millie was hoping that the security men wouldn't be picky.

'Meanwhile, me and Max—'

'Max and I,' corrected the cat.

Millie gave him a hard stare, and then grinned.

'Max and I,' she repeated, 'will run to the main doors. Ah. What's going to happen with the power?'

'My brother's doing it.'

'Your brother? Does he work for the electricity company?'

'Not exactly. He's doing it from home.'

'How?'

'He's hacked into their grid. He's really good at that sort of thing. You'd never know he was . . .'

'He was what?'

'Nothing. He's hacked into their system, anyway. Call him when you need the power cut, let it ring three times, then hang up. Have you got a phone?' he asked.

Millie waved her mobile at him.

'Great. Here's his number. It's pay as you go, so it can't be traced.'

'Good.' Millie keyed the number into her phone.

'We should swap numbers as well,' Jake added, and they did.

'So, when you run off with the guards, we call your brother and hang up after three rings. That's the signal to cut the power to the alarms and the cameras, but not the doors. Has he isolated those?'

'Of course.'

'We go through the main doors. We get up to the third floor, and then the airlock doors will still open, because the power to them stays on.' Millie felt she had to go over everything step by step, in case she'd forgotten something.

'Once the cats are free, they run down three flights of stairs and into the woods, from which point, they're on their own,' said Millie rather sadly.

Jake frowned.

'They wouldn't want it any other way,' Max assured them. 'They will want to be alone after all this time cooped up in jail.'

'Then we make a run for it, too. But if there's any time at all, we'll try to get some proof of what's been going on from Arthur Shepard's office, which is here.' Millie shone a faint beam of light on the map and pointed at it.

'But if we can't get it, it doesn't matter,' said Max. 'We're not going to get caught doing it.'

'Agreed,' said Millie. But her eyes burned at the prospect of letting Shepard get away with it. 'Is everyone ready?' she asked.

'Ready,' said the other two.

'Then let's go to work,' she said, flicking off the torch.

A few hundred yards away, Arthur Shepard's ears should have been burning, were there any truth in the old wives' tale. He was still in his office, even though it had gone eleven o'clock at night. He was waiting for a van to arrive at eleven fifteen, to ship the cats off to another laboratory in Lincolnshire where no one would find them – at least not for a while. Not until it didn't matter, anyway. He had been at work since dawn finalising these arrangements and smoothing things over with his boss, another rich yet unpleasant men, and he was extremely tired and cross. He looked at the clock on the wall and felt his eyelids droop, simply too heavy to stay open much longer.

*

A few miles away, an unmarked white van turned merrily down a small road which the driver erroneously thought would lead him to the Haverham laboratory. He would drive several more miles before he realised his mistake, performed a U-turn, and drove back to the main road to try again.

Chapter Twenty

Jake and Millie agreed to stay in telephone contact throughout the evening. Millie wondered if they should have prearranged a signal to let the other one know if they were caught, but she hadn't wanted to suggest it, in case she jinxed the mission, so she stayed quiet. If she didn't hear from Jake at all for four hours, she decided, she'd call the police. Surely the most trouble they could get into was for trespassing and being a nuisance? Millie felt cold at the thought of what her dad would say if he found out that she'd been lying to him, wandering the countryside in the middle of the night and trying to break into a building.

They edged to the very outskirts of the forest, only a tiny distance away from the lab, almost exactly where Millie had first seen the man and his crate of cats. Jake ran off, hoping to bump into the security men on their rounds. Millie and Max stood poised, until their muscles ached. Nothing. What if they were doing their rounds *inside* the building, rather than outside? How would Jake draw them away then? After what felt like a thousand minutes, there was a sudden explosion of noise: a large dog barking; a man shouting; and Jake yelling nonsense at the man and racing off into the distance, taking the guard with him.

'This is it,' hissed Millie.

Max's ears had gone flat on his head when he heard the first bark, and he jumped into her bag, a plan he had rather unwillingly agreed to for the sake of speed – although he could outrun Millie over short distances, he wasn't used to running very far at a time, and they planned to go straight through the doors and up three flights of stairs. Millie dialled the number Jake had given her, waited for it to ring three times, and hung up. She looked at the building, hoping she would see something happen. Seconds later, the few lights on inside went out and, almost immediately, a second set came on. Millie guessed they were powered by an emergency generator. She just hoped the cameras weren't as well, but she reasoned that some lights would have to stay on in any building, in case of fire. Cameras didn't really help in a fire, unless you had a special passion for grainy video footage of burning buildings, so she felt a little reassured. Millie pulled up her hood on the off chance she was mistaken, thinking that if the CCTV *did* capture her, Shepard might think he was being robbed by a midget, not a twelve-year-old girl. She ran as fast as she could to the front doors. As she peered in through the glass, the lobby seemed to be empty. None of the cameras was moving, although they only changed direction every few minutes, so that didn't necessarily mean she was safe. She expected the doors to open as she approached them, but they stayed resolutely shut. The outer doors must be on the same circuit as the cameras and lights, she reasoned. The only other possibility – that Jake's brother had made a mistake, and that the airlock doors upstairs wouldn't open for her either – didn't bear considering. She was sure the outer ones would open manually. Who knew she'd been paying so much attention in last term's fire safety lecture? So she pushed on the doors.

They didn't move.

'The other way,' hissed Max, from her bag.

Millie took a quick, deep breath, trying to focus her brain. She pulled the doors sideways, and they were inside.

Upstairs, the noise of the dog barking almost woke Arthur Shepard, as he slept the sleep of the unjust. And the sound of the emergency generator firing into action might have woken him too, if it weren't for the fact that it was a floor below, on the other side of the building. The lights going off and coming almost immediately back on merely made him murmur something incomprehensible. But he just, just about, slept on.

The driver of the white van pulled a mobile phone from his glove box. He had followed the map that had been faxed over this afternoon as best he could, and he was still lost. His sat-nav appeared to think that he was in the middle of nowhere and had stopped offering suggestions several miles ago. He would ring for further directions. He was dialling the Haverham area code when he paused, remembering just how obnoxious Arthur Shepard had been that afternoon when he'd called to arrange the pick-up. No – he wouldn't give that jumped-up little beggar the chance to be rude to him again. He snapped the phone shut. He would just have to be a little late.

Millie and Max had already decided that they would go up the nearest stairwell. Now Millie raced up the three flights of stairs. She was breathless by the time they reached the second floor, panting uncontrollably by the time she wrenched open the fire door on the third.

'You ride that bike everywhere,' said Max, still sitting happily in her bag, peering over the side. 'How come you're so unfit?'

'Different muscles. Plus your extra weight,' she gasped. 'Now, which way?'

'Straight ahead,' said Max. 'At the end, turn left.'

Millie followed his instructions and came to a door which looked like an airlock in a continental bank.

'Is this it?' she checked, as she reached out her hand to press the button.

Max nodded.

She pressed the button, and nothing happened.

Chapter Twenty-One

'Damn,' said Millie. She picked up the phone and redialled. She left it for three more rings and hung up again. Then she pressed the button again, and nothing.

'What is it?' asked Max.

'I don't know,' she whispered, sounding agitated. 'I don't know if the power isn't on, or if there's a security pass we need, or . . . I don't know.'

She pressed the button again, praying for a different outcome. Still nothing. They stood for a moment, wordless, neither of them wanting to give up, and neither of them knowing what to do. Millie had bitten her lip so hard it was bleeding. Suddenly, her phone lit up. Jake's brother was calling in silence. The screen flashed once, twice, three times, and went black.

'Maybe that's the signal,' said Max, hoping out loud.

Millie reached out and pressed the button one last time; the door slid smoothly open. Millie ran inside, and they waited for the first door to shut before she pressed the second button.

Millie felt like a mouse caught in one of those humane traps – utterly powerless, completely visible and at the mercy of someone she had never even met.

'I hope he knows what he's doing, this brother,' said Max, giving voice to her fears.

'Me too.'

The door shut automatically behind them, and she pressed the next button.

The second door drifted weightlessly open.

'*Yes!*' Millie felt the way she imagined footballers must feel when they scored a goal, but only whispered her delight.

She looked around the pristine white room, the walls of which were lined with cages: each contained a cat. There were black cats, white cats, a few beautiful tortoiseshells, and one malevolent-looking orange cat. Nothing Max had told her had prepared her for this – each cat was in a small, cramped wire box, lying on newspaper. They had water bowls, food bowls and nothing else, not even a bed or a scratching post. They barely had room to stretch out. It was bad enough that they had been kidnapped, operated on, and changed for ever, but surely there was no need to keep them in these conditions? The wire was a fine gauge, as though the lab techs expected the cats to be able to squeeze through anything more than a quarter of an inch wide. Millie had no doubt as she ran forwards that these were the same cages the unfortunate rodents had been kept in, before the cats arrived. Clearly nobody had thought that an animal five times the size of a rat might require five times more space – they had simply jammed the bigger creature into the same miserable prison. She found herself hating Arthur Shepard and his helpers more than she would ever have believed possible. Furiously, she put her bag on the table in the middle of the room and began opening the cage doors.

'Who are you?' asked a grumpy voice.

'It's me,' said Max, jumping from Millie's bag onto one of the tables in the middle of the room. 'I've come to get you out.'

'Max?' said fifty voices at once. 'Is that you?'

'Of course it's me,' he replied casually. 'I said I'd be back to get the rest of you.'

'You brought a little girl along for our big rescue?' said the huge orange cat, with a nasty sneer on his face.

'She just broke into a guarded laboratory, made it up to the third floor without activating the cameras or the alarm and opened the electronic doors, so let's not start calling her names.' Max was getting increasingly sniffy on Millie's behalf.

'What time is it?' The orange cat was obviously in charge here.

'Er . . .' Millie looked at her watch. 'Twenty past eleven.' She couldn't believe it was still so early – the last few minutes had felt like hours.

'What are you doing? Hurry! He should be here by now.' The orange cat spat at her.

'*Who* should be here?' Millie was fumbling over the catches, going as fast as she could.

'Shepard.'

'*What?*' Millie and Max both jumped, staring at the ginger tom in horror.

'He knows something's up. He thinks someone knows we're here. I imagine that would be you,' the cat said in an infuriatingly calm tone now he had their undivided attention. 'We're all to be moved tonight. He was due here at eleven fifteen.'

'Arthur Shepard is in the building? Oh no!' Millie was opening the last few cages, although her fingers felt like rubber. The cats were massing on the floor, stretching their stiff limbs and yawning. She wished she could feel so calm.

'OK, we won't try his office for paperwork, then,' said Max, consoling.

'You think?' Millie's eyebrows were sky high. 'We need to go *now*.' She addressed all the cats. 'There's a corridor in front of you when the door opens. Run down there, turn right – we're going down the stairs at the end of that. It's down three flights and across a lobby, then through the doors to outside. There's a man out there with an Alsatian.' Fifty tails went upright. 'But he's chasing our colleague, so hopefully that'll be fine,' she finished hurriedly.

The orange cat looked extremely scathing.

'*Hopefully?* This is the best plan you could come up with?'

'Yes,' said Max firmly. 'You can stay here if you prefer.'

'No, no,' said the cat airily. 'I'll come.'

'Is everyone ready? We all need to get in here at once.' Millie pressed the door button and the door slid open again. The cats all piled in behind her, in a frankly undignified scrum. Millie was pleased to see the ginger cat take a paw in the face in the confusion. 'Is that everybody?'

'Yes,' said Max, doing a quick head count. Then, 'No.'

Millie looked at him in alarm.

'Where's Monty?' he said, looking round, trying to catch the face of his friend.

'Monty is not here,' said the orange cat. 'Now hurry.'

'What do you mean he's not here?' asked Millie.

'He's dead,' said the orange cat, supremely unconcerned.

'*Dead?*' cried Millie, as Max stared, completely at a loss.

'He refused to cooperate with them. They stopped feeding him. They stopped giving him water. He was already old. He died.'

Millie felt Max stiffen by her feet.

'They *killed* him?' he asked, uncomprehending.

'Yes—' said the orange cat, who was about to continue before two other cats appeared to feel the need to sit down urgently on his head.

'Max, we have to hurry,' said Millie. 'I'm so sorry.'

'He left you a message, Max,' said one of the tortoiseshells. 'He knew you would come back.'

Max turned to face her, tears in his eyes. Millie was on the verge of crying herself, but adrenaline was pumping around her body and she couldn't lose focus now.

'Celeste, what did he say?' asked Max, so quiet now that Millie could barely hear him.

The tortoiseshell cat gazed at him. Her voice shook a little. 'He said to tell you that you were *my* rescuer, but not his. That he didn't want to live with what they had done to him. That he was sorry he couldn't stay to tell you himself, but that your escape was the only thing he had enjoyed this past year. He said to wish you luck.'

Max nodded very slowly. 'I'm sorry we couldn't be here sooner,' he whispered.

'He knew you couldn't,' she said. 'So do I.'

'Max, I have to—' Millie looked down at him and took a deep breath. She pressed the second button, but the inner door remained firmly open, and the outer one just as firmly shut.

'Squash up more,' she said desperately. 'One of you is keeping the door from closing.'

There was a peevish *meow* from someone, and the door clicked shut. The second door now finally opened, and they ran full tilt down the corridor and around the corner. As one, the cats suddenly stopped and stood rigid in the dim light.

Millie ran as fast as she could to reach the cats, and almost tripped over a straggler as she rounded the north-west corner, trying not to tread on any paws or tails as she crashed to a halt.

'What is it?' she gasped.

'Shh,' snapped the ginger cat. 'Someone is coming up the stairs.'

Chapter Twenty-Two

The van driver had eventually cracked and rung Arthur Shepard, who was annoyed on several counts: first, with himself for having been asleep; second, with the driver for having woken him up; third, with the driver again for being late. At the very moment the great escape was racing down the west side of the building, Arthur Shepard was heading up the stairs on the south-west corner to put all the cages on a trolley and take them down to the ground floor in the service lift for when the van arrived.

Millie thought her heart would burst into her throat. She looked frantically for Max to confirm what the other cat had said.

'He's right.' She heard his voice, even though she couldn't see him. 'Turn back.'

They raced back the way they had come and around to the far set of stairs, where Millie had collected all the rubbish bags. The fire door was shut now, so the cats couldn't escape as easily as Max had when he fled the first time. Rather, they had to wait impatiently, twisting and writhing like a multi-tailed, fluffy hydra, as Millie ran to catch them up.

'Whenever you're ready,' muttered the orange cat.

Millie was now certain that this must be Ariston, the cat who used to pick on Max.

'Sorry I'm slower than you,' panted Millie, 'but at least I brought my opposable thumbs.' The cat frowned in annoyance, as Millie leaned on the door handle. 'Now *run*!' she said. 'I'm right behind you.'

They raced down the stairs, Millie taking them two at a time to try and keep up with the pulsing carpet of fur. She reached the ground floor, and stopped.

'Wait,' she whispered. 'I'd better look around first.'

The cats backed away from the door, and Millie opened it a crack. She and Max peered round it. The corridor which led towards the lobby looked empty. She couldn't see the *whole* lobby from here – that was why they had preferred the other staircase. Well, preferred it until they realised Arthur Shepard was using it, anyway. She was sure that the front doors would be shut, as they expected. She dialled Jake's brother one last time, and let it ring three more times, to signal that the doors needed to be unlocked again, and the cameras and alarms must remain turned off. They all waited, paralysed in silence, every second thinking that the door above them would open and that Arthur Shepard would find them, trapped at the bottom of the stairs. Millie felt sick from the tension. She swore to herself that after tonight she would never do anything again that involved waiting for someone else to do something – it was the most wretched sensation in the world. Her phone flashed once again. She looked around one final time and then glanced down at Max. He nodded.

'Go,' she said.

The door swung open and every single cat erupted simultaneously into the corridor, following Max to the lobby. They weren't quite at the doors when the unmistakable sound of a curdling shout of rage came from the third floor. Millie and Max eyed each other nervously. The automatic doors remained stubbornly shut until Millie wrenched them apart a few inches. She held the doors open as the cats raced past her to get outside.

Suddenly Max hissed, 'Millie – move!'

She frowned at him – half the cats were still waiting their turn to cram through the doors.

'Now!' he shouted.

And finally she saw the headlights of the van which Max's pricked ears had heard seconds earlier, driving up to the front of the lab. She looked down in horror at the remaining cats, let go of the doors, and ran back into the lobby, hiding behind the security man's desk. Max was there even before she was, but there were still eight or nine cats milling hopelessly by the closed doors.

'Hide,' Millie whispered urgently, peering round the side of the desk. Perhaps they couldn't hear her, or perhaps they were too confused by the huge, empty space in which they found themselves, after so long cramped up in cages – but they seemed paralysed, gazing out at the unexpected lights. 'You'll be caught,' she begged. 'Please, hide.' But it was too late.

The van driver was walking up to the doors, just as Arthur Shepard flew down the staircase that Millie and Max had originally planned to use, panting heavily from the exertion of running down three flights of stairs. Millie ducked back behind the desk, flattening herself against the chair so her reflection wouldn't show in the huge windows.

'Ah,' he said, with a savage glee. '*There* you are. Well, *some* of you.'

The cats looked around in panic, recognising their captor from his recent visits to their room upstairs. Arthur Shepard, meanwhile, appeared to have used the very last of his energy in this short speech and he leaned against the doors, breathing hard. Millie was relieved – they were only a few feet away, and if he weren't making such a noise himself, he would surely hear her heart beating as though it was about explode from her chest, like the alien in the film her dad didn't think she had watched.

'Yes, here I am, mate. All of me,' said the van driver rather tartly, misunderstanding Arthur Shepard's words and assuming (since he could see no one else nearby) that Shepard was talking to him.

'What?' snapped Shepard, who had apparently not even noticed the man standing outside.

The driver, in turn, had not noticed the cats as his gaze was fixed on Arthur Shepard's face, which was puce with fury and the unexpected exercise.

'You don't look well, mate,' said the driver, with a total lack of concern in his voice. 'Need some air, by the looks of it.'

'What?' said Arthur Shepard again. He was still too out of breath to say much more.

'Doors broken, are they?' asked the driver.

'Yes,' piped up a voice, which was not Arthur Shepard's. 'Give us a hand with them, could you?'

Millie never did know which cat had spoken, but one of them had come to his senses with excellent timing.

'Here you go,' said the driver. And he pulled the doors open with ease, making Millie blush to think how she had struggled to do the same.

'No!' cried Shepard. '*No!*' The last of the cats ran between his legs to freedom, as he reached down, grabbing at them. He caught the tail of the last one and lifted it triumphantly in the air. 'Got you,' he crowed, grabbing it by the neck so it couldn't bite. 'Don't scratch,' he warned, tightening his grip. The cat went limp.

'*No!*' whispered Max. 'He has Celeste.'

Millie placed a hand gently on his back. This was no time for heroics.

'You idiot! Try and catch them!' Shepard cursed at the driver. But the cats that had made it through the doors had disappeared like smoke on a windy day, dispersing in every direction, as though they had never been there at all. The sound of mocking laughter echoed back from the woods, growing fainter every second.

'No need to call people names,' said the driver, now rather huffy. 'You asked me to open the doors. Should have made sure your cats was in cages, shouldn't you?'

Arthur Shepard gave the man a look of pure, undiluted hatred. 'Chase them!' he demanded.

'Chase cats, in the dark? You're joking, mate,' said the van driver, sounding happier at having something concrete to refuse. Shepard looked around desperately.

'Where's the dog?' he continued.

'You've lost a dog as well? Dearie me, you *are* careless,' said the van driver helpfully.

'The security guard's dog,' snarled Shepard. 'Did you see anyone as you drove up?'

'No, mate,' said the driver. 'Who else have you lost?'

'I haven't lost *anyone*,' said Arthur Shepard, his voice shaking with anger. 'People have broken into my laboratory and stolen most of my cats. You just lost the rest. They've only just left the building. You must have seen them. They must have driven past you to get out of here.'

Millie could scarcely breathe. What if he realised they hadn't left the building at all? He only had to walk a few feet, and he would be standing right over her and Max.

'Didn't see anything come past me. There must be another route out of here, mustn't there?' said the driver. 'If I'd known I was in charge of your security as well as driving your cats halfway up the country, I'd have been paying more attention, wouldn't I?'

Shepard fixed him with a glare. 'Go away,' he said, so quietly that Millie could scarcely hear him.

'Are you sure?' asked the driver. 'Because I'm supposed to be picking up a consignment of cats . . . No, hang on, you've lost 'em, haven't you?'

'I *said*, go away,' Arthur Shepard's teeth were gritted.

'Right you are, mate,' said the driver, feeling and sounding perkier than he had done all day. And he got back into the van, slamming the door. The engine started up and he drove swiftly away.

Shepard went slowly back to the stairwell, no doubt, thought Millie, to take Celeste straight back to the lab. She and Max had to be quick, so she texted Jake's brother silently.

are the cameras still off?

The reply came back immediately.

yes.

'We have to go,' she said to Max. 'I'm so sorry.'

He nodded, saying nothing. And they moved silently towards the doors.

*

That was it. They were free. She turned to look back at the laboratory as they ducked into the woods. They had made it. They ran a few feet into the cover of the trees, and then she stopped, picking Max up to carry him through the darkness. He still said nothing.

'I'm sorry,' she said again, and he finally turned to look at her. Tears were streaming down her face.

'You don't look very beautiful when you cry,' he said softly.

'Sorry.' She wiped her eyes and nose on her sleeve.

'That, of course, is much more lovely.' He gave her a half-smile, and patted her gently on her less grimy arm.

'We'll get her back,' Millie promised. 'I just don't know how yet.'

'You will,' said Max. 'You will.'

Max guided Millie effortlessly to her bike, and they began the journey back across the fields towards town. They had only gone about a mile, however, when Millie felt the bike lurch beneath her.

'What is it?' asked Max.

'Puncture,' Millie replied. She was suddenly exhausted, as though all the night's stresses had caught up with her at once. She stopped pedalling and began to dig through her bag, hoping, rather than expecting, to find a puncture repair kit.

'Can you fix it?' asked the cat.

'No,' she sighed. 'A repair kit is the one thing I forgot to bring.'

'You also forgot tissues,' Max added helpfully, staring pointedly at her sleeve.

'It's one of the two things I forgot,' she conceded. 'I'm afraid it'll be a slow walk home. You can sit on the saddle, though.'

They began to trudge wearily over the fields, Millie's bike lights providing just enough illumination for her not to lose her footing.

She looked down at Max and thought what a miserable evening he must have had – first, the news about Monty, and then losing Celeste. She didn't really know what to say, so she decided to start with the obvious.

'I'm really sorry about your friend Monty,' she began.

'Don't be.' Max gazed up at her and blinked slowly. 'He was an excellent cat. Clever, dignified and stubborn. He punished them the only way he could, and he paid the price for it. But it is what he chose to do – I'm sad for myself, because I shall miss him very much, and for Celeste, because she has lost her father. But I cannot be sad for him. He did what he thought was right.'

Millie nodded.

'We'll make them pay for it,' she whispered.

'Yes,' said Max. 'Yes, we shall. By rescuing Celeste,' he finished grandly, rather spoiling it by adding, 'Again.'

Millie nodded. The plan to rescue Celeste might have to

come tomorrow, she thought. She was just too tired to think of something now.

'Do you think Jake made it out of there all right?' she said, suddenly remembering their partner in crime. She realised rather guiltily that she had quite forgotten about him in all the excitement.

'I hope so,' said Max, who had also failed to give Jake a moment's thought since they'd heard the Alsatian pursuing him at the start of the rescue. 'Should we call him?'

'I don't know,' said Millie, frowning as she pushed her bike over a small trench. 'I mean, there's no way he'd be home by now, is there?' She looked at her phone, checking he hadn't left a message, and noting with astonishment that it was still only midnight. Had it really only been an hour since they saw him run off into the night? She supposed so. 'Depending on how far he was chased, he's got to get back to wherever he left his bike – at least, I guess he has a bike.'

Max nodded slowly – they knew almost nothing about the boy. 'He'll probably call you when he gets home, wherever that is,' said the cat, reassuring.

'Mmm,' said Millie, hoping he was right.

It had been a long evening for Jake, too. He had led the security guard away from the building with ease. Jake had outrun him and his Alsatian by some distance, mainly because the man had appeared to believe that panting, 'Oi, you! Stop!' was an effective security measure. Jake had gone way past the lab and into the woods before doubling back to the main road, once he was sure he'd lost his pursuers for good. He'd hopped over the fence and waited by the side of the road for a while, in the hope of catching up with Millie and Max later, and seeing the rest of the cats.

He had still been sitting by a bush on the grass verge when a van, with the unmistakable air of being driven by someone who'd lost his way, had pootled past him. Jake had ducked behind the bush, and hidden until the van went out of sight. Ten minutes later, the van had come back again. Frowning, Jake had watched it retrace its path, and then turn uncertainly into the laboratory driveway. He had sworn under his breath. He'd vaulted back over the fence and sprinted towards the lab. He had to warn Millie. What if the van was going after her and Max? Maybe someone had tipped them off. He had tugged his phone from his pocket and tried to call her. The screen had flashed at him instantly, telling him it had no network coverage. Jake had sworn again. Then he'd thought for a moment, wondering what he should do.

He'd almost made it back to the lab, so he pressed himself against the back of the building, hoping that he'd be able to hear what was happening without being seen. He'd held his breath as he'd watched the driver climb out of his van. He had been standing there, leaning against the wall, motionless and silent, for several minutes, just as Millie and Max were crouched behind the lobby desk only a few feet away. He hadn't been able to hear what was happening at all, but he'd been almost sure he had seen a couple of dark, cat-sized shapes run past him, melting into the black undergrowth. He'd strained to see the driver get back into his van, without Millie, Max or any other cats, so far as he could see. He'd waited a few minutes more, hoping to see Millie leave safely. Suddenly, he had heard a shout, 'Oi! You again! You wait right there!'

Jake had rolled his eyes, and started to run again. This time, he'd gone straight back to the main road, now he knew he could get over the fence easily enough. The Alsatian had barked delightedly, seeming to think this was a new game arranged especially to alleviate his considerable boredom. Jake had launched himself over the fence and across the road into the ditch on the far side, where he'd left his bike earlier. He had lain there for a few minutes, panting hard and trying to get his breath back. He'd jumped in surprise as he felt fur brush past his head.

'Wha—?'

'Sorry,' a cat had said, in a perfectly modulated voice, as though he were reading the evening news. At least, Jake assumed it was a cat – he could see nothing in the darkness except two huge green eyes, staring at him. 'And thank you, by the way. That was a splendid distraction. Very good indeed.'

'Er . . . you're welcome,' Jake had replied, still not fully comfortable with a cat talking to him, even when it was complimenting him.

'I'm afraid I must be off,' added the cat. 'Really, though – thanks. Marvellous work.'

Jake waited for a few more minutes, wondering if he dared head back into the laboratory grounds a third time and risk the chance that the Alsatian had now learned the rules of the new nocturnal race. He looked at his phone, which now winked a signal at him. He hadn't missed any calls or received any texts. So maybe Millie and Max were OK? He would text them, just to check. As he began to type the message, he heard another engine. He peered through the foliage, and saw a car's headlights racing down the driveway from the lab. He shoved the phone back in his pocket and picked up his bike. Whoever it was could have Millie and Max prisoner, and the thought made him go cold. Had the mission been a failure? He would follow them. The car drove right past him, only a few inches away, and he felt a rush of relief – he was certain he hadn't seen Millie in the car. Unless she was a prisoner in the boot. Jake leaped onto his bike and began to give chase. He slammed his feet onto the pedals, and kept up with the car for perhaps half a mile before its powerful engine took it around a bend and out of sight. Cursing again in frustration, Jake only then realised that his bike lights were still in his pocket. He had been using the car's headlights to guide him, and now he was in total darkness. Two seconds later, he was lying in the ditch at the side of the road once again, on top of his smashed phone and broken, battered bicycle.

'Ow,' he muttered.

As they continued to walk, past the fields and now on roads at last, Millie thought about the cats they'd managed to release.

'Where do you think they all went?' she asked.

'I don't know,' Max admitted. 'There were only a few who were native to Great Britain. The rest came from Belgium and France.'

'Do you think they'll be OK?'

'Of course they will. They are cats, self-reliant by nature. They will hide out here for a while, try to find some soft-hearted people to adopt, or they will head home.'

'How would they get home?' Millie was mystified.

'By boat? Or, more probably, by the Eurostar, I think. Less water.' Max shrugged.

'You think they'll get the Eurostar home?' Millie looked at him suspiciously, convinced he must be teasing her.

'I think perhaps this exercise is affecting your brain. Yes. They will get the train to Calais or Brussels, and they will make their separate ways home from there.' Max said it matter-of-factly, as if the cats were no different from business-men returning home from an overseas conference.

'But how would they get through customs?'

'Easy. They are not carrying anything illegal.'

Millie now looked at Max very hard.

'Oh, I see,' he continued. 'You mean, how will they get through *unnoticed*?' He gave her a proper smile, the first since they had found out about Monty and lost Celeste.

'Well, yes. Given that they won't have tickets. Or passports. Or, you know, be people,' Millie added, as she smiled back.

'You think the train is just for people?' Max was amazed.

'Isn't it?'

'Of course not. They will go to Waterloo, they will hide among people's bags and cases. They will sneak on board once they have been carried through customs.'

'What about the X-ray machines?'

'What about them? The cats aren't carrying guns. They may not even have luggage.'

'Well, it'll pick up their bones, won't it? You'll see the skeletons of cats going through the machines.'

'No, they will go through the metal-detecting part, like the people do.'

'You seem to know a lot about this.'

'Well, we discussed it a lot in the laboratory. How we would escape from there, how we would get away to London, or the coast, how we would get the train or a boat and arrive home. Between us, we knew quite a lot.'

'So I see.' Millie thought this quite an understatement. 'And what about you?' she asked in a small voice.

'What *about* me?' Max was confused.

'Don't you want to go home?'

He gave her a long, even look.

'Yes,' he said finally.

'Oh.' Millie pressed her lips together, trying not to cry for the second time that evening. These cats were an emotional business.

'Ah, Millie, don't be sad.'

'OK.'

'No, I don't mean just stop being sad. I mean you *shouldn't* be sad. I'm not going home straight away. Not until we have rescued Celeste, and then exposed this man, this Arthur Shepard.' Max spat out his name. 'And then I was hoping you might help me to get home. To be honest, I was hoping you'd come with me, and help me to explain everything to Sofie and Stef.'

'OK.'

'It's not OK, is it?' asked the cat shrewdly.

'Not really. I'm sorry. I mean, I know it's your home, and of course you want to get back there. It's not like you ever wanted to leave.'

Max shrugged, casually, as though being kidnapped were only a small inconvenience for a cat of his stature.

'I suppose I just like having you around. I've got used to it. I'll be bored without you.'

'Of course you won't be bored. Surely there is some industrial espionage you need to be getting on with,' suggested Max.

Millie giggled. 'You're probably right.'

'Besides, you will be back at school soon, won't you?'

'In September, yes.'

'Well, think how bored I would be, waiting around for you to come home and entertain me every day. Haverham is not as exciting as Brussels for exploring, you know.'

'Well, think how bored *I'll* be every holiday without you to muck up my plans of sitting around and feeling sorry for myself. In Haverham, which is not as exciting as anywhere,' she pointed out.

'You will have no time to do that, then, either. You will have to come over and visit me.'

'Really?'

'Of course really. You will like Sofie very much. And you will like Stef too, I'm sure. You will definitely come to visit.'

Millie wasn't sure if he was asking her or telling her.

'OK.' She leaned over and scritched Max behind the ears. And they walked on.

Chapter Twenty-Three

They were not too far from Millie's house now, and there was still no word from Jake.

'Maybe I should ring him?' Millie wondered.

Max shrugged. 'Is that wise?'

'I could text him,' she thought out loud. 'No, I can't. They'd see my number. I mean, if he's been capture— If he doesn't have his phone any more,' she rushed, unable to say aloud what they were both thinking. She hoped he hadn't been caught by the security man. Or, worse, by the Alsatian.

'I could do it from a phone box. No,' she corrected herself again. 'They could track us to the phone box.'

'Do you need me to contribute to this conversation, or are you happy having it with yourself?' asked Max, in tones of some exasperation. He was very fond of Millie now, but sometimes she was a bit hard to follow.

'Sorry. You know, I'll text his brother. I should have thought of that in the first place.'

She really was tired, thought Max. So was he. He watched as she texted quickly with just one hand, still pushing the bike along with the other.

Is Jake OK? We haven't heard from him.

Moments later, the reply came:

Go home. Will call tomorrow. He's fine. Bit bruised.

'Oh dear,' said Millie. 'He's bruised, apparently.'

'It's not as bad as being bitten,' Max pointed out, ever the pragmatist, particularly where large dogs were concerned. He was a little suspicious of Jake, anyway, after he had lied about bringing a mass of people to help with the rescue. He knew that Millie had done pretty much the same thing, but he already trusted her, and knew that she hadn't had much choice. Jake's brother had done very well, admittedly, with the electricity and everything, but Max couldn't shake the feeling that if Jake had brought more help, Celeste would not now be in captivity again. He changed the subject, not wanting to share these thoughts with Millie, in case she thought he blamed her, too, for the loss of Celeste.

'Where are we going, by the way?' he asked.

Millie looked surprised. 'Home,' she said. 'Aren't we?'

'No, we can't,' said Max.

'Why not? Oh, because Dad thinks I'm staying over at Sarah's?' she asked.

'Exactly.'

'I think he was going to stay over at a friend's, too,' Millie said, with a slightly nauseated expression.

'Really?' Max raised his eyebrows. This was a side of Millie's father he knew nothing about.

'Yeah. There's a woman Bill introduced him to that he has the occasional fling with, when he thinks I'm not around to notice.' Millie sounded very casual, almost as though she had been practising.

'Ah,' nodded the cat sagely.

'She's a bit annoying. I think that's why nothing serious has come of it,' confessed Millie.

'Ah.' Max nodded again.

'Ah, what?'

'Ah, nothing. He is a man. It is allowed.'

'I know. It's a shame she's not, you know, better, though. Then he could actually have a proper girlfriend,' Millie said rather sadly.

'Better at what?' asked Max, confused.

'Better at anything,' she replied, rolling her eyes.

The woman had obviously made quite an impression, thought Max, but he was too sensible to say anything other than, 'Ah.'

'Oh, shush. There's only so much manly wisdom I can take from a cat.'

'Sorry.' But Max didn't sound very sorry. He sounded as though he thought it all rather funny.

'Anyway, let's get back and find out. We'll come up with Plan B if we need one,' she finished.

*

Finally, Millie pulled her bike up onto the lawn and wheeled it around to the back of the house. The gate squeaked a little as she pushed her bike through, but it couldn't be helped. It wasn't loud enough to wake anyone up. She went to the back door and peered in. The house looked deserted. There was only one way to be sure, though. She walked softly around to the front and put her key in the bottom lock. Sure enough, it turned. She undid the latch as well and they crept inside.

'Thought so,' she said. 'He only locks the bottom one if we're out. And you can't double lock the top one except from outside.'

'Good,' said Max. 'Let's go and get some sleep. It must be two o'clock.'

'Pretty much,' she replied, looking at her watch as she went to the stairs. 'Actually . . .' She went back to the door and relocked the bottom lock. 'Since we're here on our own,' she added. Max nodded, and they disappeared upstairs to get some sleep, after what had been a very long day.

Chapter Twenty-Four

Arthur Shepard was undone by fury. Someone had broken into his laboratory while he was here, while he was downstairs, no less, waiting for a useless damned idiot to drive a van here and collect these pestilential cats. How had the intruders got through the doors? How had they known where to go? How, in fact, had they known there were cats here at all, unless they had the escaped one? That was it. He seethed with rage, tiny spots of foam fizzing on his lower lip. Either the cat had run away and found someone to help it steal the others, or those sodding window cleaners had done it. He stormed up to the third floor and into the laboratory. He hurled Celeste into a carrying cage and locked the door.

'Ouch,' she hissed at him, her eyes turned to slits.

'Shut up,' said Arthur Shepard, 'or I will *make* you be quiet.'

Celeste realised that this was not an empty threat and sulked at the back of the cage. Shepard marched back downstairs, the cage swinging precariously from his hand. He stomped into his office and slammed the cage down on the floor. Celeste hissed again.

He picked up the phone to call security to set them onto the problem. Then he remembered once again that security should have been guarding the outer perimeter of the building. How had these thieves got in undetected? Didn't he pay these men decent money to stop just such an eventuality? The answer to this question was, of course, no. He paid them dreadful money and thus had useless security guards like Dave.

Now Arthur Shepard dialled Dave's number three times, making mistake after mistake as he tried to press the correct buttons while shaking with anger. The first number was unavailable. The second number he called turned out to belong to an irate fireman, who was trying to get some sleep, and called him a lengthy list of names before explaining helpfully that were his (Arthur Shepard's) house to catch fire, he would have only himself to blame if it burned to the ground because he (the fireman) would be too tired to come and put it out, on account of having been woken up by idiots (Arthur Shepard) in the middle of the night. Arthur Shepard apologised insincerely, which was the only way he knew, and tried to call Dave again. He thought he had misdialled a third time when the phone was answered by someone apparently having a severe asthma attack.

'Hello? Hello?' he snapped.

'Hello, sir?' gasped Dave, who had his head between his knees, like a much fitter man who had just completed an Olympic sprint.

'Dave? Is that you?' Arthur Shepard resented having to call this man 'Dave', as though they were friends. He would have much preferred to call him 'David', indicating formally that they were employer and employee, but the stupid man never remembered to reply if called by his correct name, as he claimed to be known universally by the abbreviation, and simply did not think of himself as a David.

'Yes, sir.'

'Where the devil are you?' Arthur Shepard could barely contain his fury.

'Outside, sir. Near the road. I saw some teenagers mucking around and chased them off.'

'When?'

'Sorry, sir?'

'When did you see these teenagers?' asked Arthur Shepard, sounding more and more annoyed.

'Ooh, must be half an hour ago, sir. At least. Maybe longer. They led me a right chase, running around the building and off up the road. They're gone now, though, sir. No trespassers here anywhere, I've checked.' Dave was still panting feverishly, wondering if he should take a little more exercise these days. He belonged to a gym, but had seen no more of it than the inside of the café and, unaccountably, that seemed not to have helped his fitness levels the way he had expected it to.

'Excellent work, Dave,' said Arthur Shepard, through thin lips.

'Thank you, sir.'

'Yes. While you were chasing ne'er-do-wells about the grounds, you left the building unguarded – wide open, in fact – and there has been a break-in.'

'What? Sir?' Dave began to panic. His job wasn't usually this difficult.

'Oh, be quiet. And, incidentally, you're sacked.' Arthur Shepard hung up the phone irritably, thinking that all this could have been averted if the security guard hadn't been so stupid. He didn't think, even for a second, that perhaps the responsibility might lie with him for having paid for only one guard to look after a large building. He certainly didn't think about the fact that he had been in the building himself as it had been breached, yet he had heard and done nothing. He wished, briefly, that he had employed more than one man on the night shift, but only because that would have brought the satisfaction of having more than one person to fire now. Firing people was probably the only part of Arthur Shepard's job that he actually enjoyed. He would have really liked to fire the van driver, and he felt a festering annoyance that he had been unable to do so, because, sadly, the man didn't work for him. Perhaps he could persuade someone else to fire him tomorrow.

Arthur Shepard realised he needed to regroup. He would have to take the remaining cat away from this laboratory – the security here was compromised. He thought for a moment, then dialled a number he knew off by heart.

'Hello? Hello, yes, it's me,' he said. 'I'll be with you in half an hour.' He paused, listening. 'Yes, there's a problem. I need you to look after something for me.' He paused again. 'Yes. No, I don't know for how long. See you later. Bye.' He hung up and began to think.

He knew two things. One, that one of those window cleaners was responsible, at least in part, though he couldn't prove it. His protesters had kept all other undesirable animal rights types away from the lab and they had fed him information about the only person who had seemed to see through them – some boy who had nothing like the brains to pull this kind of thing off. Besides, people had broken in to free the cats – it *had* to be someone who knew they were there. And the most likely candidates by far were the window cleaners – they were the only people who had been on the premises when that mangy grey cat had escaped. This meant he needed to call Mickey and Ray, and get them out of bed and round to the houses of the two window cleaners straight away, to see if they could find out if there was anything going on. He made another abrupt call and arranged this. One of them would go to each house, to save time.

The second thing he knew beyond a doubt was that his

security cameras would have picked up this whole sorry mess. By the time his men were in their cars, speeding towards the little suburban houses he was sure that the window cleaners lived in, he would have checked the tapes and would know how many people were involved. He realised that it was most likely they would have had accomplices to help them break in – maybe journalists. He was always reading in the papers about some undercover hack who'd broken into a supposedly secure building – Buckingham Palace even. God, it didn't bear thinking about. But he would be able to see their faces, if they hadn't realised the cameras would pick them up – he might be able to get them arrested before they could publish anything about him. He would go straight down now to the CCTV room and view the tapes himself. He would call his men with new information in ten minutes. Maybe less. He walked quickly, not seeing, in the dark, the trail of paw prints which would taunt him the next morning as he retraced the cats' steps. He crossed the lobby, pulling a ring of keys from his pocket. He thrust one of these into the CCTV room lock and began feverishly to check the camera footage from that evening. As he found the correct tape, he wound it back and played it. Inexplicably, the picture was blanked out for all the vital minutes. For the second time that night, a howl of inarticulate fury rang out around the laboratory.

Chapter Twenty-Five

Millie couldn't sleep, even though she was exhausted. Her brain couldn't stop whirring through the events of the night – the lucky escape they had had, the panic she had felt when the laboratory doors wouldn't open, the near capture by Arthur Shepard, and how on earth she was going to rescue Celeste. She turned over and tried to think about something else.

She woke with a start seconds later. She looked at the clock and found that it really was only five minutes since she had last checked it. Max was sitting bolt upright, his ears rigid.

'Someone's trying to get in through the front door,' he hissed.

'What?' Millie jumped out of bed. The noise had been too quiet to wake her up, but now she was awake, she too could hear the unmistakable sounds of someone trying to unlock the door.

'What shall we do?' she whispered. 'Hide?' She looked

around frantically. The house wasn't really designed for secret hiding places.

'No. Bluff,' said Max.

'What do you mean, bluff?' she asked, as the noises continued from downstairs.

'Turn on the lights,' replied the cat calmly.

'What? Are you insane? They'll know we're here.'

'Exactly. We want them to think we're here. And other people too. Lots of them. Now hurry. Turn on the lights and shout to your dad that you've had a nightmare.'

Millie's eyes narrowed and she nodded. She opened her door and flipped on the light.

'Daaad,' she howled. '*Daaad!*'

The scratching at the door stopped abruptly.

'Dad, there's someone in my room. I'm sure there is. In the wardrobe.' She was wailing like her life depended on it. She hoped it didn't.

'What?' shouted Max, in his deepest, most English-sounding voice. 'Don't worry, love. It's just a bad dream.' He pulled a face.

'It isn't! I saw them,' she cried again.

'Millie, shush. You'll wake Sarah and her parents,' he bellowed. 'I knew I shouldn't have let you girls watch a scary film.'

They listened carefully and heard nothing. Then a few quiet steps. Max was poised to jump onto the windowsill to see if the man was leaving, but Millie put her hand down, warning.

'He'll see your eyes,' she said.

Max nodded. She really was a smart girl. Cats' eyes reflected far more light than human ones, he knew. And his eyes were bigger and oranger than most other cats' eyes.

Millie slipped through to the spare room, where the curtains were open, and crept on all fours to the window. She peered over the ledge, and saw a large man get into a car, start the engine and drive away without lights on. She ran back to her room and picked up a pencil.

'W202 FYF,' she said, scrawling it down.

'Sorry?' Max was confused.

'The registration number. Of his car. In case we need to give it to the police.'

'Ah. Very clever.'

'Not as clever as you, giving us a houseful of guests. How quick was that?'

'Thank you.' Max preened.

'I think you should let us watch another horror film tomorrow, though. You're such a square. All the other dads let their daughters do it.' She grinned at him.

'Shush.' The cat rolled his eyes in mock exasperation.

'Sorry.' They started to laugh, as a night's worth of tension finally caught up with them both.

'Are you still tired?' Millie asked.

'No. Maybe . . . I think I am hungry.'

'Me too.'

They went downstairs and Millie made toast, her solution to virtually any crisis that didn't require three-dimensional building plans and minor law-breaking. Max ate some cat food in a half-hearted way and, eventually, they went back to bed.

Then at eight o'clock, her phone began to ring.

Chapter Twenty-Six

It was Jake's brother's number on the screen. Millie picked it up and said nothing, just in case.

'Is that you?' asked Jake.

'Is that you?' she asked back.

'Yes. I mean, it's Jake. I'm using my brother's phone.'

'It's Millie. Are you OK?'

'I'm fine. Well, a bit bashed up. Did you get them out?'

'Yes, all except one,' said Millie. 'We have to find her and get her back.'

'Right. OK,' said Jake.

Millie thought perhaps she *did* like him. There was something to be said for a person who simply agreed with you when you proposed a second rescue mission that would almost certainly involve further criminal activity. Particularly if they had been injured in the first one.

'Are you badly hurt?' she asked, realising she should probably have mentioned this sooner. 'What happened?'

Jake told Millie about his exploits the previous night, and Millie explained about the near misses with Arthur Shepard and the van coming to collect the cats.

'Oh, that explains it,' said Jake. 'I took down the registration number of the van, in case they'd kidnapped you too. And I got the number of the car that left just after it.'

'That must be Arthur Shepard's,' said Millie. 'It's his lab.'

'I wrote it down while I was lying in the ditch, waiting for my leg to stop twitching.' Jake seemed quite proud of this. 'So we should be able to find out where he lives.'

'How?'

'The police and the driving licence place have reverse directories. You type in the car registration and it gives you the home address.'

'How will we get into those?'

'My brother can do it.'

'Really?'

'He's a pretty good hacker. I mean, he tries not to draw attention to himself by doing MI5 or the Vatican or anything, but he's pretty good.'

'OK. Well, here's another one for him.' Millie gave Jake the number of the would-be intruder, and told him what had happened when she and Max had got home early this morning.

'Wow.' Jake was impressed. 'You two are pretty hardcore.'

'Thanks,' said Millie. 'I would slightly prefer it if no one was trying to break into my house in the middle of the night, though. I mean, I could stop being hardcore quite easily.'

'Come round later,' said Jake, 'when my parents are at work, and we'll see what we can find out. Maybe we can get enough to give to the police. Or the papers. Then Shepard won't have time to be sniffing around you and Max.'

This sounded like an excellent idea.

Jake gave her his address. 'Come round at ten – Mum and Dad will be long gone by then.'

Millie agreed, hung up and told Max the plan. 'I'll leave a note here for Dad. She looked at the clock, considering. 'He's gone straight to work, I guess, from what's-her-face's house.'

'Is that her real name?' asked Max innocently.

'Yes. It's on her birth certificate, next to a surprisingly late year,' said Millie acidly. 'Now, let's have breakfast, and then I'll fix that puncture.'

Chapter Twenty-Seven

As Millie reached up to ring Jake's doorbell, the door swung softly open on its own.

'Come in,' muttered Jake, from behind the door.

'What's going on?' asked Millie suspiciously.

'Nothing, really.' He reached behind her and pulled her bike inside, propping it up against the wall. 'I just thought you might be being followed.'

'I don't think so,' said Max, his head popping out of her bag like a well-trained magician's sidekick. 'I've been keeping my eyes open. We haven't seen that man, or his car. And I didn't see the other man either.'

'What other man?' asked Jake. Max could be quite confusing, he thought.

'The one I watched search Millie's house the other day.'

Max jumped down onto the carpet. Millie looked at Jake properly for the first time, and saw that he was holding his left arm awkwardly. His long-sleeved T-shirt concealed a bandage.

'I fell quite hard,' Jake confessed, seeing concern in her face. 'I've twisted my left knee, and I think I've sprained my elbow – it's the size of a melon,' he added, sounding reasonably proud of this fruity achievement. And now Millie looked closely, his arm did seem to swell out in the middle.

'Ouch,' she said.

'I know,' he sounded rueful. 'You should see my bike.' He pointed out of the hall window and Millie saw a mangled bicycle leaning against the wall like a crippled crane fly.

Max jumped up onto the sill and had a look for himself. 'Oh dear.'

'I know. I dunno what I'm going to tell my parents,' he sighed. 'The truth, I suppose.'

Millie looked extremely surprised.

'Not all of it,' he explained. 'Just the bit where I fell off. Not the bit where I was following a guy in the dark without my lights on round the unlit roads outside of town, after acting as a diversion for two burglars.'

'I should leave all those parts out,' agreed Max. 'No point worrying them if you don't have to.'

'I hope I didn't worry you two, either.' Jake looked apologetic. 'I tried to call you, but there was no signal for a while. And by time I had a signal . . .' He paused awkwardly. 'By the time I had a signal again, my phone was in three separate pieces,' he finished.

'Can you fix it?' asked Millie sympathetically. She would

be lost without her phone. It had been on her top ten list of things not to forget before attempting the break-in, along with maps, food, quiet shoes and Max.

'Not a hope.' Jake shrugged.

'Never mind,' she said. 'I forgot my puncture repair kit, so we had to walk home.'

'She forgot tissues, too,' said Max.

Jake shook his head sadly. 'Dear dear,' he said. 'You forgot tissues. What a shambles. I dunno how you managed to break in anywhere with that kind of slacker attitude.' He grinned at them both.

'I have a question,' said the cat. 'Why did you try to follow Arthur Shepard at all and get into this mess' – he nodded at Jake's bike and his many injuries – 'if you can simply get his address from your, what is it, reverse directory?' Millie had told Max all about this on their way over.

'I didn't know I could then,' explained Jake. 'That was another one of my brother's bright ideas. He mentioned it this morning.' He shrugged wearily and then winced.

Millie was just about to ask about Jake's elusive brother, when they were interrupted.

'Are they here? Are they here?' called a child's voice from upstairs.

'Who's that?' asked Millie.

'This is Ben,' said Jake, as a small boy appeared at the top of the stairs.

'Hello, Ben,' said Millie.

'Hi,' Ben said shyly, looking down at the cat. 'Is this Max?'

'Hello,' said Max.

'He really talks!' Ben was delighted, a huge grin splitting his face in half. 'Come on up.'

'Are you sure you should have told your little brother about us?' Millie tried to sound less annoyed than she felt. The more people who knew about this, the more danger she and Max, and maybe her dad or even Bill, might be in.

'Er . . . he already knew,' Jake mumbled.

'How?' she demanded.

'Well, you know, from helping us yesterday.'

'How did he . . .?' Millie's voice trailed off as Max's jaw dropped.

'*That's* your brother? The computer hacker?' She was horrified.

'Yeah.' Jake sounded embarrassed. 'He's a lot cleverer than people think. I mean, he's way cleverer than me. He has an IQ of 168. He's a genius, really.'

'Your baby brother did all that yesterday?' asked Max, who looked as shocked as Millie felt, which was some consolation.

'He's not a baby. He's nearly ten.' Jake was getting defensive.

'I'm glad you saved this information till now. To think you were so rude to Millie about being a "little kid".' Max glared at Jake.

'Well, who knew she'd be exactly like him?' Jake sounded genuinely affronted. 'I spend half my time being told what to do by one child genius. I didn't realise she was another.'

Millie blushed.

'Anyway, he got you in, didn't he?' asked Jake.

'Yes, he did,' Millie conceded.

Max shook his head slowly from side to side. 'I can't understand it,' he puzzled. 'I spent years of my life thinking children were simply noisy and sticky. I get kidnapped, I escape, and every child I meet is some kind of master crook. Millie is like an arch-villain, plotting away with her nerves of steel, you are able to elude large dogs and disappear at will, and your brother apparently controls the electricity supply for this entire area.' Jake shrugged modestly, and Millie blushed again. Max continued shaking his head. 'I am either the luckiest cat in England or this country is populated entirely by unusually gifted children with criminal tendencies. And yet, you all look so innocent . . .'

'Come on,' shouted Ben, poking his head over the banister above them. 'Jake says we've got another cat to rescue. And then we're going to nail the bad guys.'

Millie raised her eyebrows briefly.

'He likes those American police shows,' said Jake.

Max and Millie nodded mutely.

Chapter Twenty-Eight

If Millie's room had seemed to Max to be a good place in which to plot an escape, Ben's room could have belonged to an international criminal mastermind with an unusual fondness for cartoons. Computers, scanners, printers and web-cams all gleamed on a huge desk, beneath a giant poster of several animated superheroes on the wall. The computer had already been in action and printouts littered the table.

'Here are the registered owners and addresses of all the vehicles you saw,' said Ben, waving them at Millie.

Obviously Jake had also reported back. She scanned them quickly.

'So, the van that came to pick up the cats belongs to a company in Lincolnshire.'

'It's a front. Another testing lab,' said Ben.

'How do you know?' asked Max.

'I ran the company name through a search to get the

names of the directors. Then I searched for other companies in their names. That's where I found this.' Ben handed them another bit of paper. It was a copy of the home page of an animal research centre.

'That's theirs, too.' Millie nodded as she read.

'So the orange cat—'

'Ariston,' supplied Max.

'Ariston?' asked Jake. 'What kind of name is that?'

'Apparently, it means "The Best",' scoffed Max. 'We always said it should stand for "Best at Annoying Every Other Cat in the Room".'

'Well, it pains me to say it, but "Ariston"' – Millie rolled her eyes – 'was right. They were being shipped off to another lab. Lucky we went when we did. And lucky you saw the van and got the registration. There's no way Max and I could have seen it without getting caught.'

Jake smiled proudly.

'And the guy who came to our house last night was . . .' Millie leafed through the sheets Ben had given her.

'. . . Ray,' finished Jake.

'He works for Arthur Shepard directly, not through Vakkson,' offered Ben.

'How do you know that?' This was far more information than Millie had managed to unpick from the net.

'He runs a security firm. Pretty scuzzy one, though.' Ben handed her another sheet of paper. 'It says they offer security for people and property. But Vakkson uses a different company for their site security – this one.'

Ben brandished another sheet, and Millie recognised the colours of this home page – they were exactly the same as the uniform of the security man who sat at the front desk – maroon and grey. She began to laugh.

'You're amazing,' she said.

'Well, Jake helps,' he replied, trying and failing to look modest.

Jake nodded, and pulled a face.

'Yup,' he said. 'I load the paper into the printer. And sometimes, I staple things together.'

'So we know all about the van and the heavies. And that just leaves . . .' Millie reached out and took the last sheet. 'Arthur Shepard's home address?'

'No.' Ben was irritated. 'His car's not listed to his home address. It's listed to a business address, and that turned out to be a mailbox, not a real place at all.'

Millie pressed her lips together in annoyance.

'Sorry,' said Ben.

'Don't be sorry.' She felt guilty now. 'It's not your fault. We'll just have to think of another way to find out where Shepard might be keeping Celeste. I don't think he'd have taken her to his house, anyway. He's very secretive about his business dealings, isn't he? I can't see him taking Celeste home – his neighbours might see her.'

Max looked worried.

'We'll think of something, mate,' said Jake to the cat.

'We will,' promised Millie.

'So, what next?' Ben had obviously had more sleep than the other three put together and was bursting with energy.

'I don't know,' said Millie. 'I was hoping we'd be able to get proof of the cats being held in the lab when we raided Shepard's office. But then he turned out to be in the building, so we just made a run for it.'

'You did the right thing,' said Jake fervently, and rubbed his sore arm again.

'Hmm. We still need to find an answer to the most basic question,' said Ben.

'Which is what?' asked Max.

'Which is, who wants talking cats?'

Chapter Twenty-Nine

'We've tried to figure this out before,' explained Millie. 'But we couldn't find anything online and we couldn't think of any reasons ourselves.'

Ben looked pained – he hated failure. 'I've tried too,' he admitted. 'There's nothing, is there?'

'Not that I could find. But you're better at this kind of thing. I mean, how did you do that stuff with the electricity last night?'

'Oh, it was easy. Their electricity grid was hardly protected at all. And the different circuits weren't even encrypted. They'd practically labelled them. If they'd put the cameras and the doors on the same loop, that would have been tricky, but honestly, it was as if they *wanted* someone to break in. I turned the cameras back on after you'd left, by the way. Just because it was funny.'

Millie grinned at him. She wondered how funny Arthur Shepard had found it.

'But I can't find anything that connects Vakkson to cat research at all. They usually deal with rodents.'

'Mmm. That's what *we* thought. But Max doesn't reckon there were any other animals in the building.'

'If there had been mice, I would have smelled them,' he said patiently. 'Mice, birds, little helpless voles – cats know.'

The others nodded.

'So, if they aren't doing any rodent research at Haverham,' said Jake, 'is it anything to do with Vakkson at all? Is the cat thing Arthur Shepard's pet project?' Millie, Max and Ben all stared at him. 'Sorry,' said Jake. 'That pun was unintentional.'

'It's a good question, though,' said Ben, tapping away at the keyboard, flicking through page after page of information, his eyes barely seeming to scan the screen before he dismissed it and moved on.

'I don't know,' he said at last. 'Vakkson don't seem to be doing anything in this country.'

'Nothing at all?' asked Jake.

His brother shook his head.

'Well, why do they have a lab in Haverham, then?' Millie asked.

Ben frowned and typed some more.

'They don't, really,' he exclaimed. 'They used to have a department here, then they moved operations to Germany two years ago. They tried to sell it, but there were no takers, so they've leased it out.'

'He is even more alarming than you, Millie,' said Max, looking at Ben with awe.

'They leased it to Arthur Shepard?' she asked.

'Yes.'

'So this *is* his . . . private project,' said Jake. 'But why does he want to make talking cats?'

'I've tried to remember everything I heard while I was there,' said Max. 'But the technicians didn't seem to know anything. They hardly spoke to us at all, except to ask us stupid questions about whether or not we felt nauseous.'

'Well, let's think.' Millie was frowning again. 'It's going to cost a huge amount of money to rent a building that size, isn't it?' They all agreed. 'And you were there for at least a few weeks?' she checked with Max, who nodded his head. 'And you weren't the first cat there? So some of them might have been there for a few months?' He nodded again, his long, grey whiskers waving as he moved. 'And,' Millie continued, 'Shepard's paying for separate security, well, house-breakers, on top of the guards who look after the building, who are paid for by Vakkson?'

'That explains why that guard was so useless – Vakkson probably use good people for places which they actually *use.* All they need for a lab they're renting out to someone else is a bloke to make sure windows don't get broken, or squatters don't move in,' said Jake.

'And he's paying for the technicians . . .'

'And he has a really nice car,' added Jake.

'So it's probably a big company that's bankrolling him, but not Vakkson, do we agree?' asked Millie.

Everyone nodded. Then they all stopped, realising they had come to a dead end.

Chapter Thirty

'Did none of you see *anything*? Anything that might give us a clue?' Ben asked.

'Nothing,' said Jake.

'No,' said Max.

They all looked expectantly at Millie.

'The only thing I did see . . .' She trailed off. It was too stupid. She had checked it once and found nothing. But it was the only thing she could think of that had been out of the ordinary. 'There was a newspaper in the rubbish,' she said. 'They lined the cages with paper, which I think is why it was there. Only, it was missing its middle pages, and I thought someone had taken them out to read them – it was just one big sheet, you see, which wasn't enough to line a cage with. So I thought maybe there was something important in the paper, and that's why they'd kept it away from the cats.' Millie carried on, aware that Ben and Jake were looking increasingly underwhelmed: 'And I checked it at the library, but I think it was just a picture they'd taken out. Only, why take the whole page?'

Ben twisted his mouth as he thought. Jake patted Millie on the shoulder and said, 'You know that just because they can talk doesn't mean they can read, don't you?'

Max pulled a huffy face, and failed to mention that he wasn't much of a reader himself yet.

'Which newspaper was it?' asked Ben.

'*The Times*,' said Millie, surprised he was taking it seriously enough to ask.

'Mum and Dad get that,' said Jake. 'What was the date?' he asked.

'Erm, about three weeks ago,' she said, as she struggled to remember.

'Jake!' exclaimed Ben. 'Have Mum and Dad taken the papers to be recycled yet?'

'Don't be silly, little bro.' Jake ruffled his hair. 'Have you heard an almighty crash as Europe's largest paper mountain collapses to the floor of the garage?'

'Not since about May,' admitted Ben.

'Then the papers are all still there, aren't they?' said Jake. 'Why do you ask?' Ben gave him a hard look. 'Oh,' Jake grinned. 'I see.'

They traipsed out to the garage and gingerly approached the leaning tower of papers. They took them carefully from the top, trying not to damage the infrastructure of this impressive piece of engineering. Max remained out of harm's way, as he rightly suspected that if this pile of paper collapsed, he might never be seen again.

'How came the council don't collect your paper?' asked Millie. 'They take ours every week.'

'Mum and Dad never remember to put it out, till there's so much the council won't take it,' replied Ben.

'Sometimes we think about doing it, to save them the trouble,' added Jake cheerily. 'But it just encourages them.'

'That's it,' said Millie, as they reached the edition that she had fished out of the rubbish. 'Here.' She flipped through the pages until she found the middle sheet.

'Phwoar,' said Jake, looking at the large picture on the front.

'Urgh,' said Ben, poking his brother in the ribs. 'She looks like a giraffe in a dress. And that's not even really a dress. It's more like string.'

'Well, that's why the page was taken out,' said Jake simply. 'I'd have taken it myself if I'd seen it.'

'There must be something else,' said Ben, turning the page.

'That's what I thought,' said Millie. 'But if there is, I don't know what it is.'

Ben scanned the business pages, just as Millie had, shaking his head in disappointment as he finished reading.

'Well, I'm still taking this upstairs,' he said.

*

They all read and re-read the missing pages.

'Share prices,' Jake moaned. 'What do they even mean?'

'It's how much a company is worth, I think,' said Millie. 'The share price is high if lots of people want to buy them, and low if no one does. People want to buy shares in companies that are doing well – you know, selling lots of stuff, or whatever.'

'What do they buy from telecom companies? What do they sell?' asked Jake.

'I have no idea,' she admitted. 'But, see, this company, Playmatic' – she pointed to a brief article about a toy and games manufacturer – 'their shares are worth less, because they've lost their director. He's left, and taken some of their best-selling toy ideas with him. See, it says that they're trying to sue their lawyers, for letting him have a contract that. . .' Her voice petered out as she noticed that Jake's eyes had glazed over. He came to with a jolt.

'Sorry,' he said. 'Were you still talking?'

'She does that a lot,' sympathised Max, thinking of how he had felt when Millie tried to explain computer security to him.

'I don't get that,' said Ben.

'Really?' asked Jake, cheering visibly.

'No, I mean, I understand it,' said Ben. 'I just don't *understand* it.'

'Oh,' said Jake.

'I mean,' said Ben, loudly, 'why would Playmatic not be worth loads? They make the Plastidroids. Those are so cool.'

'Plastidroids . . .' Millie murmured. 'Those bendy robot things?'

'They're just the best,' agreed Ben. 'I wanted one so badly last Christmas, but you couldn't get them any . . .' He stopped talking, distracted by Millie's expression. She suddenly looked as if someone had switched on a light in a dark corner of her brain.

'What is it?' asked Max, who had noticed this as well.

'Arthur Shepard had one,' she said. 'In his office, when I was there. On the filing cabinet. Why would he have a Plastidroid?'

'Present for one of his kids,' said Jake promptly.

They all stared at him.

'Does he have children?' Max asked in some horror.

'Yup,' said Jake. 'Three, aren't there?'

Ben absent-mindedly picked up a sheet of paper with 'Confidential Census Information – Do Not Print' written across the top.

'Urgh,' said Millie. They all shuddered. 'Anyway, I don't think Arthur Shepard is the kind of man to buy presents for his kids, do you?'

'No,' said Max.

'So, why did he have a Plastidroid?' asked Ben.

'Could we look up Playmatic?' asked Millie.

Ben began to type. 'Here we go,' he said.

'What does it say?' asked Jake.

Millie summarised: 'Playmatic's share price has gone way down, even though they made the coolest toy in the world last year.'

'Why?' asked Max.

'They underestimated demand,' explained Ben. 'It says here that they made about a hundred thousand droids. The writer reckons they could have sold ten times that many in this country alone.'

Millie took up the story again. 'So then the men who run the company had a meeting and decided to fire the director. They blamed him for messing things up. They could have made loads more money if they'd made more toys.'

'I see,' said Max.

Ben had now read another article and said, 'The director was forced to leave, even though the Plastidroid was his idea. And when they got rid of him he took his idea with him, and now he's set up another company to make them for this Christmas.'

'They let him take their best-selling toy with him when he left? Surely they would have been better keeping him *and* the toy?' asked Max, thoroughly confused.

'I'm glad you're here,' whispered Jake. 'Normally I'm the one asking stupid questions.'

Max raised his eyebrows infinitesimally, then remembered that Jake had sustained an injury helping him to rescue his friends and lowered them again.

'No – well, yes.' Millie was very excited. 'That's what the thing was about in the paper. His contract should have prevented him from taking any ideas away if he left. Or even working for any other toy company for ages—'

'Five years, minimum, it says here,' said Ben, who was still reading happily as he spoke. 'But some lawyers messed things up. Look, there's a quote from a spokesman at Playmatic. He says they're going to have the best Christmas toy ever this year. He says no one's going to want anything except what Playmatic is bringing out. Apparently, they're going to make Plastidroids ancient history.'

'They have Plastidroids in ancient history?' asked Jake. 'I thought it was just Romans and sandals and stuff.' Ben looked at him in disgust. 'Sorry,' he finished.

'That's far stupider than what I said,' Max pointed out.

Jake sighed. It was true.

'What will the new toy be like?' wondered Ben, tapping eagerly on the keyboard. Several minutes later, he still looked puzzled. 'Hmm. It doesn't say anywhere.'

'Let's think about that later,' said Jake. 'Why did we even start talking about this?' He was regretting having brought up the fact that he didn't understand share prices.

'Arthur Shepard,' said Millie. 'He had one of the robots in his office. They were virtually unobtainable – Ben couldn't get one, nor could anyone else I know. So how did he get one? Could he have contacts at Playmatic?'

Ben scoured the internet again. 'I'll be a few minutes,' he said.

'I'll go and get some food,' said Jake. 'Anyone else hungry?'

Max's ears pricked up and Millie nodded – they hadn't eaten for hours. She and Max went down to the kitchen with Jake. Max was delighted to discover that Jake's parents weren't vegetarian and had a fridge well stocked with ham and cold chicken. Millie and Jake made sandwiches and took one upstairs to Ben. He was concentrating too hard to hear them come, it seemed, because suddenly he shouted, 'Jake!'

'Aahhh,' said Jake, dropping the sandwich on the floor. 'Don't shout!'

'Sorry,' said Ben, picking the sandwich up off the carpet, dusting it off, and beginning to eat, his eyes never leaving the screen. 'I've found it,' he said.

'Found what?' asked Jake.

'Playmatic has been paying Arthur Shepard hundreds of thousands of pounds a month,' said Ben, hopping up and down with glee.

'You're kidding,' said Millie, racing over to look at the screen. 'I wonder if *he* took that page out of the newspaper. I guess he's probably quite interested in their share price, if he's working for them.'

'Excuse me,' asked Max. 'Is that Arthur Shepard's bank account that you two are looking at?'

'Mmm,' said Ben. 'This bank should work a bit harder on its security if you ask me.'

'Yes, I agree,' said Max.

'They're paying him *how much*?' asked Jake.

'Two hundred thousand pounds a month. Some of which goes to Vakkson, some to the security men, a big chunk to some other people who, I think, must be the lab techs, and about a quarter he keeps,' said Millie, reading quickly.

'So what does that tell us?' asked Jake. 'I told you I always have to ask the stupid questions,' he muttered to Max.

'It tells us that Playmatic are very confident that their new toy is going to be a huge hit,' said Millie. 'So confident, they're investing a fortune in it.'

'And Arthur Shepard is involved? What is the new toy?' asked Max.

Millie looked at Ben, her eyebrows forming a question. He nodded slowly.

'Well, don't take this the wrong way,' said Millie. 'But you are.'

Chapter Thirty-One

Max's fur bristled like a force-nine gale had just passed through the room.

'*What?*' he said softly.

'I said, you are,' Millie repeated. She looked at him, her brow creased with concern. 'I'm so sorry,' she said, realising as she spoke how feeble she sounded.

Ben and Jake looked embarrassed, both feeling that they were intruding on a private scene. Max was still rigid: his tail, his fur, his ears were all pointing at the ceiling. Millie just couldn't think of anything else to say. Max hadn't been stolen by someone trying to find a cure for cancer or a treatment for Alzheimer's, and even if he had been, she would still have found it appalling. But this was so much worse than anything she had even considered. He had been stolen to make a toy, a disposable plaything for spoiled children and their loathsome parents who thought that an animal was no different from a plastic model that you controlled with an aerial and a battery pack. Millie was suddenly deeply ashamed to be human.

'Maybe I'm wrong,' she said hopefully. 'Maybe—'

'You're not wrong,' said Jake. 'It's the only explanation that fits, isn't it? Playmatic are paying money to Arthur Shepard, he's using it to hire a laboratory, where they're operating on stolen cats and giving them voices, for no other reason we can think of. And at least two of us are really smart, so if you two can't think of it, it's because it isn't there to be thought.'

Millie looked slightly confused, but Ben had had more practice at following Jake's trains of thought.

Jake went on: 'Playmatic wouldn't invest money in this for a laugh, would they? They're a business, and a business in need of some help, from what we've read. Why else would they be paying Arthur Shepard, and what other interest could they possibly have in animal experiments? It's not like they're bringing out a line of cosmetics, is it?' He looked sternly at Millie, who couldn't think why – she didn't own so much as a lip-gloss. Sometimes, she couldn't even find a hair-brush.

'But who would want such a horrible . . . not that I'm calling you horrible,' Jake added hastily, trying to placate Max, who didn't seem to be really listening to what he was saying anyway. 'Who could possibly want . . .?'

There was a long pause.

'Me,' said Ben.

'*What?*' Millie and Jake were shocked.

Max still sat in total silence.

'Shut up, Ben,' said Jake, flushed with embarrassment.

'No, I mean, I wouldn't want Max to have been kidnapped. I wouldn't want him to have been brought miles away from home and kept in a cage; I wouldn't want him to have been operated on without his consent; I wouldn't have wanted that to happen to any of the cats, even Ariston, and he sounded horrible. I just mean, if I didn't know all that, if Playmatic had just announced in November that you could have a talking pet, I would have wanted one more than anything, more than a Plastidroid, more even than a really cool new laptop.'

'I *said*, shut up,' snapped Jake, as Millie whimpered. 'I'm really sorry about him. He's just a kid.'

'He's quite right,' said Max, so quietly they could barely hear him, especially since Ben was now crying.

Millie tilted her head, asking him a silent question. She looked like a bird when she did that, Max thought. Although not the kind he would eat, obviously. The other kind.

'He's right. That's how it would have worked, isn't it? Children love animals. They would have gone crazy for the idea of a talking cat. They wouldn't have thought about the thefts, the imprisonment, the torture; they would just have seen the most exciting pet they could ever have hoped for.'

'That's true,' said Jake, patting Millie and Ben awkwardly

on the shoulder with each hand. 'When I was a kid, I wanted a woolly mammoth, like, a miniature one. About the size of a small dog. I would have given anything for one of those, if they'd worked out a way to make them small.'

'And transport them through time,' added Ben.

'Yeah, that too, obviously.' Jake tried to look like someone who knew that woolly mammoths were extinct. He had always vaguely assumed that they lived in China or somewhere.

'But, surely . . .' Millie seemed unable to grasp it at all '. . . surely they couldn't have expected people to believe that talking cats had just appeared out of thin air? People would have realised that secret research had gone on, that these animals had been given unnecessary surgery. They would have been appalled, wouldn't they? There would have been an outcry, like there was about testing cosmetics on animals. Like there is about fur.'

'Is there?' asked Jake bitterly. 'You can buy fur in loads of shops nowadays, even in Britain, and we're supposed to be a nation of animal lovers. We once went into a department store in Paris and they had a whole fur section. We were going to take paint and throw it on them, but Mum rumbled us.' He looked at Ben, and they both eyed a state-of-the-art water pistol on one of Ben's shelves and sighed sadly at another wasted opportunity for criminal damage. 'Anyway,' he continued, 'they sell fur in half the shops on the high street now.

People aren't as high-minded as you think, Millie. If they'll wear the skin of a dead cat – sorry,' he said to Max, who nodded to show that he understood that Jake wasn't trying to be rude, 'they won't think twice about buying one that's been mucked around with, will they?'

'But' – Millie was at a loss – 'surely the cats would tell their owners that they'd been tortured?'

'You'd do it to kittens,' said Ben pragmatically. 'Operate on them when they're really tiny, too small to remember anything, and then sell them when they're a few months old. Sorry.' He winced as he caught Max's expression.

'Is there time to do that?' Jake asked. 'Between now and Christmas, I mean?'

Ben thought for a moment and nodded. 'I think so. Max is a prototype. I really am sorry.' He grimaced. 'So they've finished the experimental stage of the process.'

'How do you know?' asked Jake.

'Max talks perfectly. The other cats all did too,' said Millie dully.

'They don't need to do any more testing,' said Ben. 'They need to breed kittens. And then they need . . .' He paused and looked at Max, who gave a tiny nod. Ben sighed and continued: 'They need a production line.'

'So they *could* have kittens for sale in time for Christmas?' Jake said. 'How long does it take to make a kitten?'

They all turned to Max.

'Er . . . maybe two months?' he hazarded.

Ben clicked on his mouse. 'Was that a guess?' he asked.

'Yes,' admitted the cat, who hadn't ever thought about kittens much.

'You were right.' Ben smiled at him. 'It fits perfectly. They'll start breeding the cats at the end of this month. The kittens'll be born at the end of October. They'll operate on them in November and sell them in December . . .'

'Just in time for Christmas,' finished Jake.

'But they'd know that the cats had been experimented on, and that it was cruel. Max is the end of the process, isn't he? How many cats died in that laboratory, do you think, before they got the surgery right? How many do you think they botched?' Millie was almost in tears.

'Millie,' said the cat, jumping up onto Ben's desk, so he could look her straight in the eyes, 'other people are not like you. They wouldn't think about the ugly history, the cruelty or anything else. They would see the shiny – well, furry – new toy, and they would want it. That is how people behave the world over – they see what they want and they take it. They don't think about anything else. Animals are the same, you know – they just have fewer opportunities for kidnap and financial gain, and so on.'

Millie looked at him sadly. 'I suppose so,' she said, sounding uncertain.

'Anyway, how else would it have worked?' asked Max.

'Shepard and his friends wouldn't have done it if they hadn't thought it was an idea that would sell.'

'I know you're right,' said Millie. 'I'm just so sorry that anyone could do this to you. I feel bad being part of the same species.'

'Millie, you shouldn't feel bad. Humans are not always good. But you are a good person. And so are you two.' Max looked at Jake and Ben. 'You have risked a lot to help me, and to help a lot of other cats you hadn't even met. Some of whom weren't even grateful. One of whom was really quite rude.'

'Well, no wonder,' said Millie, who now felt so bad about everything that she was beginning to come round to Ariston's way of thinking. 'I would have been angry with me too, in their position.'

'A few people don't make a species bad. They just make themselves bad.'

'Why did you say humans weren't good people, then?' asked Ben.

'If I hadn't met you three,' said Max, 'I might have hated people too, after the past few months. But you have been kind and helpful, and now you are going to help me even more.'

'Are we? How?' Ben was eager for more plans.

'By destroying Playmatic. And Arthur Shepard,' said Millie.

'But first we must find and rescue Celeste,' Max reminded them.

Chapter Thirty-Two

'Uh oh,' said Jake, looking at the clock in the top right-hand corner of Ben's computer screen. 'Look at the time.' It was almost two o'clock.

'Oh, no,' said Ben. 'I'm afraid we can't do anything else now. Can you come back tomorrow?' He looked pleadingly from Millie to Max.

'Er . . . yes,' said Millie, confused. 'What's the problem?'

'Mum'll be home in a few minutes,' said Jake gloomily. 'The boy wonder has a piano lesson on Thursdays at three.'

Ben was a picture of misery.

'Sorry,' he said. 'I should have said I was ill or something this morning. But then she'd probably have changed it to a doctor's appointment, and I'd still have to go out.'

'Mum's a bit pushy,' confided Jake.

'Are you good at music?' asked Millie, who played the violin only slightly better than Max could sing.

'Terrible,' Ben sighed. 'I'm really, really bad. Aren't I?' He looked to Jake for confirmation.

'Dreadful,' said Jake. 'His Mozart sounds like someone being beaten slowly to death.'

Ben nodded. 'It does. And that's my best piece. I'm so sorry. Can you come tomorrow? Can you be here at ten? We'll have all day then.'

'Sure,' said Millie. 'We'll spend this afternoon trying to work out where Shepard's taken Celeste. We'd better clear off now before your mum gets back, so we don't have to answer any questions.'

'God, yes,' said Jake. 'We'd never hear the end of it if she found out that we'd had a girl round.' He went suddenly red.

'Can I take these?' asked Millie, to cover up the rather awkward silence that had just fallen over them. She picked up the pile of papers that Ben had been systematically printing out all morning.

'Of course,' said Jake. 'Have a look at it all again tonight. You'll get much more out of it than I will, and Wolfgang here will be practising all evening. Actually, I might go out,' he added thoughtfully.

'Don't blame you,' said Ben dolefully. 'I really am bad.'

Millie gathered up the papers and stuffed them in her bag. She and Max ran downstairs, Jake and Ben in tow.

'You'll come back tomorrow?' Ben said, sounding increasingly panicky, presumably, Millie thought, because he had spent the last few days helping her and Max, rather than doing any piano practice.

'Yes,' she replied. 'Tomorrow, here, ten o'clock. See you then.'

She and Max waved goodbye, and they set off on the ride home.

'Are you OK?' Millie asked Max, as she pushed her bike up to the side of her house.

'Yes,' he said, jumping out of the basket and weaving between her feet as she opened the front door. 'Can we do some reading now?'

'Of course,' said Millie, trying not to sound too amazed. She hadn't got the impression that Max was a big fan of the research side of things, since he wasn't a great reader.

'We must make a plan to get Celeste back,' he said firmly. 'The sooner, the better. That's what you say, isn't it?'

'Yes,' agreed Millie. 'It is. And you're right. We do need to get her back, and I'm sure we can work out where she is. We just need to do some thinking.'

Max nodded, hoping he looked more confident that he felt.

Chapter Thirty-Three

Millie and Max spent the afternoon going over and over the documents Ben had produced. They ruled out hiding places for Celeste, one after another. She couldn't be at the second lab, the one that Arthur Shepard had planned to send all the cats to, because they had seen the van driver leave without her. Besides, it hadn't seemed like Shepard was all that keen to do business with them after their driver had inadvertently released all but one of his cats into the wild. Millie was almost equally sure that he wouldn't have taken Celeste home. Everything she knew about Arthur Shepard made her think he would keep secrets from his family, and wouldn't trust his children an inch. She didn't have an address for him anyway, as he had proved resistant to Ben's investigations so far, so she hoped she was right. His security guards, according to Ben's research, lived with wives and children, too. Millie offered to bike past their houses, to see if she could find anything out, but Max wouldn't hear of it. He agreed that Celeste was unlikely to have been placed in a family home, without tight security. After all, they had only managed to break the cats out last night because of careful planning and a lot of help, not because Shepard had been lax in arranging security guards and cameras.

Millie chewed her lower lip in frustration. They were both pretty sure that Arthur Shepard wouldn't trust one of the thugs Max had watched searching Millie's home to look after an expensive research prototype. Even though Max hated thinking of Celeste that way, he realised they had to think, at least a little, like Arthur Shepard if they were to work out where she might be.

'I don't know,' said Millie regretfully, as she put the last page on the pile in front of them. 'Could she be with the head of Playmatic? His home address' – she shuffled through and consulted a sheet – 'is two hundred miles away. I can't see it, can you? I think he wants to keep her nearby.'

'Yes,' Max agreed. 'Also, he probably hasn't told them yet what has happened.'

'No.' Millie thought for a moment. 'No, I bet he hasn't. He'll be hoping to use Celeste in place of you all and get himself out of trouble that way. I mean, she can talk, can't she? She does what they want. He'll probably just . . .' She trailed off.

'Just what?' asked the cat.

'Just be planning to steal some more cats and set up a breeding and surgery lab somewhere else,' said Millie, looking rather queasy.

'We *have* to find her,' said Max.

They looked at each other. Millie turned over the pile of papers and began reading again from the beginning.

At two minutes past ten the next morning, Millie knocked on Jake and Ben's door. She didn't feel a great deal less tired than she had yesterday – she had slept badly again, racking her brains for any clue she might have missed that would lead them to Celeste.

Jake bounded to the door, seemingly recovered from the worst of his injuries already. 'Come on up,' he said happily. 'Ben's been awake since dawn. He could do with someone else to talk to.'

'How was the piano lesson?' asked Max, as they traipsed into Ben's room.

'Awful,' he said cheerfully. 'And over for another week. I reckon my teacher'll just take Mum to one side soon and explain to her that I'm pretty much tone deaf, and then I'll be free.'

Max nodded.

'It's a good strategy,' added Jake. 'I thought Dad might cry for a minute last night when you mangled that piece for what, the fortieth time?'

'Forty-third,' said Ben. 'Yes, he did go a bit . . .'

'Fragile,' finished Jake. 'Can't say I blame him. He likes music,' he explained to Millie and Max. 'Ben's killing him.'

'Now,' said Ben, 'it's time to get back to work, isn't it? Have you had any more ideas about Celeste?'

Millie shook her head and explained where they had got to the previous evening, which was, she felt, precisely nowhere.

'It's a start,' encouraged Jake. 'You've ruled some things out, at least.'

'We've ruled everything out,' she sighed. 'And we're all out of ideas.'

'Well, we'll think of something,' said Ben. 'In the meantime, we should go back to the original plan – to damage Arthur Shepard's credibility. And Playmatic's, too.'

'But how?' Jake was bemused. 'We haven't got any proof he's involved – Millie and Max couldn't get into Shepard's office when they did the rescue. I suppose we *could* introduce Max to the press,' he said thoughtfully.

'Max is *not* going to become part of a media circus,' Millie said, giving them a very stern look.

'Or even a media pet shop,' added Max, his mouth twitching a little.

'Fair enough,' said Jake. 'It was just an idea. How *are* we going to tell people about all this, then?'

'I don't know,' Millie muttered. 'If only we'd been able to steal some paperwork or something.'

'What kind of thing did you have in mind?' asked Ben.

'Oh, I'm not sure,' she said. 'We didn't really know even when we were planning to get into Shepard's office. I guess we were hoping for letters or emails between him and his employers, or scientists, or something about the testing. Photographs of the cats squashed in those tiny cages would have been really good, but there was no time to take any when we got into the lab. My camera was in my bag, and I was going to, but then Ariston told us that Shepard was moving them that night and we just panicked.'

'With good reason,' Max pointed out. 'We only missed him by seconds. I think it was a dignified and well-timed retreat, rather than a panic.'

Millie smiled. 'We were just too late,' she said. 'If he hadn't been in his office, I suppose we could've found some documents that connected him to the kitnapping.'

'The what?' asked Jake.

'Cat-kidnapping.'

'Oh.'

'Well, you come up with a better word.'

'No, that's fine. Carry on.'

'Well, that's it, really. That's the kind of thing we need,' she said, shrugging.

'Easy,' said Ben.

'How is it easy? Can you hack into his email and stuff?' asked Jake.

'Hmm – maybe. I think something else might be better . . .' Ben cracked his knuckles.

'I wish you wouldn't do that,' winced Jake.

Chapter Thirty-Four

Ben had been muttering with Millie for several minutes, typing quickly as they spoke. One or other of them would look puzzled for a moment, then nod and suggest something.

'It's weird, seeing him with someone who understands him,' whispered Jake to Max. 'It's like seeing monkeys talking to each other in a wildlife documentary.'

Max agreed. 'Do you think they will explain what they are doing sometime?' he asked.

'Sorry, yes,' said Ben, overhearing. 'Now, the things we know about Arthur Shepard are this. One, he gets paid lots of money by Playmatic, so he doesn't want to upset them. Two, he's not crazy about computers.'

'How do we know that?' asked Max.

'He doesn't do his banking online. There was no provision set up when I hacked in yesterday. He doesn't live anywhere near a branch of his bank – I found his address this morning, by the way, from the bank's records.' All the while he was talking, Ben was flicking through pages he'd brought onto the screen – the bank home page; Arthur Shepard's bank account; a map of where Shepard lived; a list of banks in the area. 'So it's inconvenient for him not to use internet banking. We think he doesn't use it because he's worried about security.'

'With all his bank account details, not to mention an aerial map of his home, on the desktop of a nine-year-old boy, he may have a point,' said Jake. 'I hope you don't do this to people who *aren't* international animal smugglers, thieves and crooks.'

'No, no, no,' cooed Ben. 'Of course not. I'm not sure Mum and Dad can afford to take us on holiday at Christmas, by the way.'

'Ben,' said Jake, warning him.

'Just kidding,' said Ben innocently.

'He's not kidding,' said Max.

'I know,' muttered Jake. 'He'll either be running the country by the time he's sixteen or in prison for life at the hands of the CIA. It could really go either way at the moment.'

Max nodded. Millie grinned.

'So,' she said, 'if Shepard's nervous about computers, it's probably because he doesn't know all that much about them.'

'Makes sense,' said Jake.

'Which will, in turn, make it much easier to steal the documents we need,' said Ben.

'*Steal?*' said Jake, his voice reaching a higher pitch than he had expected. 'I mean, steal?' he tried again, in a lower tone.

'Well, not steal exactly,' said Millie. 'And we wouldn't do it if we could stop him any other way.'

'We aren't going to take them off him by force,' said Ben cheerily. 'He's going to hand them over, any minute. Just wait and see.'

'I think I'm confused,' said Max. 'Why would he do such a thing?'

'Because we asked him to,' said Ben.

'Yes, I am confused,' said Max. 'Tell me again, but with different words, and more information.'

'Playmatic has a website,' said Millie, 'which is Playmatic dot com. We've checked the contact details of their staff, and their email addresses are all first name dot second name at Playmatic dot com.'

Max looked confused. A trilingual cat doesn't necessarily have a good grasp of electronic mail systems.

'So, if I worked there, I'd be Millie dot Raven at Playmatic dot com,' said Millie.

'Ah,' said the cat. 'It is clear.'

'All the emails to that address go through a server – this one.' Ben pulled up another page. 'They rent their web space and stuff from here.'

'Very well,' said Max. 'This is like the postal delivery man, yes?'

'Exactly,' said Millie.

'My head hurts,' added Jake.

'It's really not complicated,' said Ben. 'I've just hacked into the server and told them to send any mail to Nicky Browne – with an e – at the Playmatic address to me.'

'Who's Nicky Browne?' Max asked.

'We made her up,' said Millie. 'But Nicky Brown, without the e, is the secretary of the man who sends Arthur Shepard all that money every month.'

'What are the chances that Arthur Shepard has ever noticed what her name is?' asked Ben.

'Virtually none. Ask me another easy one,' said Jake promptly.

'That's right,' Ben replied. 'So, we just sent Arthur Shepard a mail from her, asking for copies of all earlier correspondence between Playmatic and him, as there's a problem with their mainframe today.'

'Their what?' asked Max, sounding a little faint.

'The thing that holds all the computers in their office together,' said Ben. 'I was hoping to hack the emails off there, but they don't store them on the server once they've been downloaded to a hard drive. More security fears, I suppose.' He rolled his eyes. 'It's stupid, though, because you have no back-ups if the hard drive is damaged.'

'They probably don't want back-ups of this stuff,' Millie reasoned. 'It is illegal, after all.'

'So you think he'll send you everything, just because you asked?' said Jake, trying to get to grips with what was actually happening, rather than what *should* happen in Ben's ideal world. He was now sounding a little faint himself.

'Yup,' said Ben. 'We don't reckon he's told them about the break-out yet. He's not had much time to, after all, and he's still got Celeste, which is probably enough. I think he'll do whatever they ask to try and keep them happy, so they don't ask him anything difficult.'

'Like, "Where are all those cats we paid you to steal and torture?"' asked Jake.

'Something like that,' Millie agreed.

'You don't think he'll be a bit suspicious?' said Jake.

'Yes, possibly,' acknowledged Ben. 'We should be emailing his secretary, really, only we don't know her full name. But the request is coming from a web address he recognises. It's a name I'm sure he'll have seen before. The only thing that's different is the spelling, and we're hoping he won't notice that. If he does, we'll need another plan. But I've already tried hacking into his computer and it's a no-go. I think he keeps it off-line, and dials up. We can try to get stuff that way, but it'll take ages. That's why we're hoping this will work.'

'So, do we just sit here and wait?' Max asked.

'Yes,' said Millie.

They didn't have to wait very long, however. A quarter of an hour later, a mail came through to Nicky Browne.

'Here we go,' said Ben, clicking on the email. He read:

> Nicky – please find our complete correspondence enclosed.
>
> Best wishes,
>
> AS

'Open the attachment,' said Jake. Max stared at him, looking surprised and not a little betrayed. 'Well, I know *some* computer things.' Jake flushed.

Ben clicked again on the inviting paperclip icon, and pages and pages of emails came up. Ben began to print them out, so they could all read them through quickly. After another forty minutes had passed, they had two piles of mail – one which proved nothing, and was therefore useless, and another which was very useful indeed.

'So, they all knew,' said Millie, who had been making lists on a notepad as she read. 'Anthony Marsden, the new director of Playmatic and his board, which is' – she consulted her list – 'seven people, plus Arthur Shepard, and the lab workers. They were all in it together. The idea came from Marsden originally – he consulted Shepard, and then persuaded the board to fund the research. We have copies of all those mails, plus reports on how many cats were used, how many died.' She pressed her lips together and carried on. 'How much they were paying and on which date the initial research stage came to an end.'

They all nodded.

'So, when we publish these, we're going to take Marsden and his board down as well,' said Millie.

They all nodded again.

'Good,' she said briskly. 'Now, what else do we need?'

Chapter Thirty-Five

On the other side of Haverham, at the lab, Arthur Shepard was pacing urgently up and down. He had kept Playmatic in the dark so far about the break-in and theft of his cats, responding to their usual day-to-day queries with prompt answers so they couldn't suspect anything was amiss. But what was he going to do? Tell them what had happened? If he did, there would be all hell to pay about the security breach, and he didn't like the sound of that at all. But if he *didn't* tell them, then surely they would soon find out anyway. The cats had been stolen, all but one of the damned things – the thieves would sell them to a journalist, no doubt.

He did have one small ray of hope – could it be that the animal rights lunatics had been the ones who'd broken in? That the intruders had not stolen the cats for financial benefit, but simply to set them free? His brain could barely countenance this suggestion, as it was inconceivable to Arthur Shepard that people would do anything for any reason other than money. Also, would the cats talk of their own accord? How stupid were they? Would they know where they had been kept? In other words, could they lead anyone back to him, or was it just the thieves that knew of his involvement? He took a deep breath and sat down at his large, walnut desk. He had a plan. He would say nothing incriminating to Playmatic, but would stall them for a few more days. He would get hold of his chief scientist, Dr Hunt, who was currently, infuriatingly, out of the country at some conference. He still had the one cat, stashed away safely at Elaine's. Thank God she didn't have any prying children to spoil things. Dr Hunt and he would soon have a new facility set up, and they would invite Playmatic to view their handiwork in a week or two, by which time they would have a few more cats in full working order.

If things went less well, and the thieves *did* go to the media, or the cats talked and the press got hold of the story, well, the worst-case scenario was that he would have to go abroad for a while, so he should probably buy an open-return ticket to somewhere pleasant, just in case. In the meantime, he needed to make sure no one could connect him directly with the project. Certainly none of the cats knew his name. He realised he needed to destroy everything on the hard drive of his computer. The research papers were all archived at Playmatic anyway, and Dr Hunt had them too, so he wasn't destroying information which he would need in the future, if the project could be picked up again as he hoped. He telephoned down to Ray, and instructed him to come to the office and to bring with him a large buzz saw. In ten minutes' time, there would be no hard drive to search.

Chapter Thirty-Six

'What do you mean, what else do we need?' asked Ben.

'Well, we need to expose them for what they've done. Do we have enough with these emails? Is there any other information we could try to get from Arthur Shepard?' Millie said.

'Nah, he'll have destroyed it all by now, even if he's a complete moron.' Ben was matter of fact about it. 'Don't worry though,' he continued. 'We'll just forge whatever else we need.'

'Brilliant,' said Millie.

'Make false documents?' Jake looked aghast.

'Yeah, of course,' said his brother. 'Well, fake images. They speak a thousand words, you know.' He grinned. 'Anyway, they won't be false. If Millie had had more time, she'd have got pictures herself. There wasn't time, because she had to escape from a horrible man, so we're going to recreate what she saw. We're doing something a bit bad. Not as bad as torturing cats, though, is it?'

'That's a very good point,' said Max.

Millie agreed and Jake shrugged.

'Being in a room with you two and my brother is like being the henchman to a trio of Bond villains,' he said.

'You like James Bond? Me too,' said Max happily.

'Then let's get on with it,' said Ben. 'This is going to be the *pièce de résistance*.'

'You don't have the vocabulary of normal nine-year-old boy,' said Max.

'You don't have the vocabulary of a normal cat,' Ben pointed out.

Max shrugged. 'Meow,' he said carefully.

'We did French at summer school,' replied Ben, grinning.

'Summer school?' asked Millie.

'He goes to a special camp for geniuses without social skills,' said Jake.

'I'm not listening. Anyway, this is the good bit.' Ben had a set of shelving units on the opposite wall from his desk which were almost cubes, with the front side missing, and they were crammed with DVDs and books. As he talked, he emptied one and said, 'Could you fit in there, Max?'

'Yes,' said the cat, looking a little bemused.

'Jake? You know when Dad fixed the fence?'

'Which fence?'

'At the bottom of the garden.'

'Yes.'

'Was there any spare wire? Could you go down to the shed and see?'

'Sure.' Jake sloped off and returned minutes later with a small piece of fine wire mesh.

'Is this enough?'

'Yup. Now, Max, you sit there.'

The cat leaped into the small space with an easy jump.

'And you two hold the wire in front of him.'

Millie and Jake held the mesh, which was more than the size of the opening, in front of the box.

'Perfect,' said Ben, as he produced his digital camera and started snapping. 'Max, could you look more unhappy?'

Max pulled a sad face, trying to look as miserable as possible. 'How's this?' he asked.

'You look really wretched,' said Millie. 'It's ideal.'

'OK, you can come out now,' said Ben, and he transferred the pictures onto his computer.

'Those are brilliant,' said Millie, as the photographs sprang onto the screen.

Max looked on approvingly.

'That's exactly how the cages looked, you know,' he said, amazed.

'Told you he was a genius,' said Jake.

'I think that's everything,' Ben said, admiring his handiwork. 'Now, how many copies do we need?'

Millie counted on her fingers: 'Local newspapers, nationals, telly – how about twenty-five of each?' she asked.

'Easy.' Ben began to print them out.

'Hang on,' said Jake. 'Can't we just email them?'

'I'm worried they'll think it's spam,' admitted Ben, 'and not read it. I'll send electronic versions too, though.'

'But there's nothing here that proves they did it.' Jake was worried. 'I mean, actually got the cats to speak.'

'We can't prove that,' said Millie.

'We *could* prove it if I spoke to the press,' Max pointed out.

'No.' She shook her head. 'They'll think it's a trick. And if they don't, that's even worse. Unless you want to spend the rest of your life doing interviews on daytime telly and celebrity pet shows.'

'Tempting, but no,' grimaced Max.

'We don't need to prove they did it,' said Ben. 'We need to prove they *tried* to do it. That's enough.'

'OK,' said Jake. 'Whatever you say.'

They made twenty-five sets of the documents and printed address labels for twenty-five envelopes. Millie and Jake would go out and post them at different postboxes across the village.

Chapter Thirty-Seven

They met back at Ben and Jake's half an hour later.

'Do you think it'll do any good?' Jake asked, looking rather doleful, as he watched Millie put her bike up against the wall, next to the mangled remains of his.

'I don't know,' she admitted. 'It's worth a try, isn't it? *I* think it's a big story, but I don't know if the press will. They might not think cats are very important. Or they might think we're crazy and just file it all in the bin. I suppose they have to check the facts before they publish anything, in case Arthur Shepard sues for libel, or slander, or whatever it's called. But he stole Max and all those other cats; he ordered illegal experiments to be carried out on them. We just have to hope that the papers go with it.'

'When do you think we'll know?'

'Well, the stuff should arrive there tomorrow, shouldn't it? So it can't be in the papers before Saturday, maybe even Monday. It could be on telly sooner, I suppose.'

They went inside and called up to the others.

'Did you send them all?' asked Ben, hopping up and down in excitement. 'I've sent the e-versions to everyone.' This was certainly the best week of the holidays, and probably the best day of his life.

'We certainly did.' Millie slung her bag onto the floor. 'What do you want to do now?' she asked Max.

'Find Celeste,' he said simply.

They had all been thinking hard about where Celeste could be, but none of them had come up with anything. Eventually, Max announced, 'I will go and look at the houses of Arthur Shepard and his thugs.'

'No,' said Millie. 'What if he sees you? He might catch you again.'

'He would never catch me,' said Max. 'I am like smoke, like mist—'

'They did catch you last time, mate,' said Jake. 'Sorry to bring it up,' he added, as Max gave him a very hard stare.

'Last time,' he said huffily, 'I was unprepared. This time, I am ready.'

'He's the smallest,' Ben pointed out. 'He'll be the hardest to spot.'

Millie looked unconvinced, but the others all agreed. Max had the best camouflage and would attract the least attention from neighbours or passers-by. They showed him a map with the suspicious houses circled in red, and he disappeared through the hedge at the bottom of Ben and Jake's garden.

Ben, Jake and Millie waited impatiently for several hours, but Max came back shaking his head. There was no sign of any of the men, nor of Celeste. He'd had a good nose around each house, and snuck into their gardens to peer in through the windows, but there was no trace of Celeste anywhere, not even her scent, which Max could have detected in a perfume factory. Regretfully, they agreed to try again the next day, although Millie admitted privately to Jake that she had no more ideas at all.

The next morning, the four of them searched in vain for any sign that their story had been believed.

'Maybe they all binned the electronic ones as spam,' said Millie. 'And the snail mail hasn't got there yet.' She knew this sounded feeble, even as she said it.

'I think the letters arrived,' said Max glumly. 'I just don't think anyone is interested.'

'Of course they're interested,' said Ben, patting Max on the head, an indignity the cat might not have tolerated from anyone else. 'They just don't know it yet. I think the problem is that we didn't think it through properly – we didn't know any journalists to send the stuff to in person. We just sent it to the offices of the newspapers and studios. We need to find someone who's interested in animal rights stuff, and get them to see what we found.'

'Good idea,' said Millie. 'Where do we start?'

They searched the online archives of every major newspaper, trying to find the names of writers who had been sympathetic to animal rights protests in the past, or who had written critically of animal testing. They came up with three names – Patricia Forsyth, Edward Davies and Scott Bradley.

'Let's send the stuff to these three,' said Millie, and Ben emailed all the evidence over to them.

'Something is definitely going to happen now,' he said, as the emails disappeared one by one.

'Still, we could do something more,' said Max.

'What like?' Ben's eyes were glinting already.

'I am not an expert in computers, of course,' began Max, 'but you found the website for Playmatic, did you not?'

'Yes,' Ben said.

'And they had many staff, only a few of whom knew about this?' The cat turned to Millie.

'Yes,' she agreed.

'Could we, perhaps, tell the remainder of the staff what has been going on?' asked Max.

Ben nodded eagerly. 'I could just send all those emails to all the staff with net access,' he said.

'I'm not sure,' said Jake. 'Would they even care? They're not going to make a big fuss, are they? I mean, they might lose their jobs if they got found out, or if Playmatic got into real trouble. I'm not saying they're all animal experimenters, but they might just not be interested.'

Millie agreed, but Max shook his head. 'Some of them may feel that what is right is more important than what is convenient,' he said rather loftily.

'It's worth a try,' said Ben. 'We'd only need a couple to make a fuss and it might start something.'

'OK,' said Millie. 'Let's make the story as easy for them as possible.'

Chapter Thirty-Eight

The four of them sat at Ben's desk, making a mock front page of a tabloid newspaper. The picture of Max in a cage was in the middle, with a banner headline, *Playmatic Embroiled in Animal Torture Scandal!*, above it. They produced a short description of the research project and Playmatic's involvement, naming all the board members and quoting the juiciest of the emails between Marsden and Arthur Shepard. Eventually, when they were all satisfied with their work, Ben posted it as the home page on the Ethical Science website that he and Jake had been running for the last six months. He mailed a link to the page to every Playmatic staff member whose address they could find.

'That should stir them up a bit,' remarked Jake, very satisfied with the morning's work. 'Let's see what happens now.'

They wanted to wait for replies, but Ben assured them that they couldn't reuse the address from which they had sent out all this mail.

'If Playmatic has even half-decent web security, they could track us down,' he insisted. 'We'll just have to hope they all go to the ES home page – I've had time to protect that properly.'

'I think we'll start seeing things happen tonight,' said Millie confidently.

And she was right.

That evening, a small piece ran in the local paper saying that a story was breaking. A major toy company and a local laboratory had been accused of stealing pets and testing them for purposes unknown. A local man was also rumoured to be involved in the project.

Arthur Shepard felt that he was running out of options, and he didn't like it one bit. In the twenty-four hours following the break-in, he had done all he could to try to put things back on track. He had saved one of his cats and made sure it was safely stored at Elaine's. He had demolished his computer and all signs of his involvement in the project. He had then sent Mickey and Ray on holiday for a few days, just to make sure they wouldn't be around if any journalists *did* find out about the cats and tried to approach them. He had spent many hours trying to contact Dr Hunt and let him know that the research project had been compromised, and that they would need to set up a second base elsewhere. He had been sure the stupid fool was at a conference in Milan, but could find no trace of him anywhere. He even went to check the personnel files for more information, before remembering that he had pulverised them with a buzz saw and they were consequently of little help.

A day or two had passed with no word from Playmatic, and no talking cats on television at all. He had begun to breathe a little deeper, feeling that things might be working out for him after all. And then, just as he was congratulating himself on victory pulled from the very jaws of defeat, his world began to cave in. The directors at Playmatic called in a furious rage, demanding to know why their staff were being bombarded with highly sensitive information about their illegal toy-development programme. He tried to explain, but no one seemed interested in his viewpoint. They just fired him, Arthur Shepard, then and there, over the phone. He still couldn't quite believe it. He had spent the last few nights at Elaine's, telling his wife that he was away on business, and now even this sanctuary seemed in jeopardy. If the story had been leaked to Playmatic's employees, it could be only a matter of hours before he was named in the media and hunted down like an animal. He now had only one choice, he realised. He pulled the air ticket and his passport out of his suitcase, his face rigid with irritation. He drove to the airport and left his car in the long-stay car park.

He thought hard about the remaining cat – was it any use to him at all? Probably not, he supposed, given how things had worked out. Maybe in another country, though . . . he might yet be able to sell it to another bidder, one less squeamish than Playmatic had turned out to be. He supposed there was no point in damaging an expensive prototype if it wasn't absolutely necessary. Still, he couldn't pretend to himself that it didn't pose a risk. He began to text:

> Cat now useless. Drown it. Don't let it go – it knows where you live.

Just because the other cats had kept quiet didn't mean this one would, after all. He saved the message as a draft – he would see how the story played out over the next day or two, and send it to Elaine if he had to.

Chapter Thirty-Nine

The next morning, the story was running on the local television news. Edward Davies, the television contact Millie had chosen, stood outside the road which led to the Haverham lab, reporting that a series of thefts and other dubious goings-on were being linked to the site. It was also on the national news, as PETA had issued a statement accusing Playmatic and their staff of crimes against animals. Even the RSPCA was threatening to investigate them.

Also, Scott Bradley, the tabloid journalist that Ben had contacted, had written an exposé on his paper's website, claiming to have snuck into the building disguised as a cleaner. Photos of cats' paw prints were featured in the article.

'This is great,' said Ben, as the four of them sat in his room, checking all the papers and watching the twenty-four-hour news channel. 'I wish we'd thought of that.'

'Yeah, good idea,' said Jake. 'They would almost certainly have let you into the building. Who couldn't mistake you for a midget cleaner?'

Ben narrowed his eyes. He'd been watching Max and picking up tips.

Millie was less enthusiastic about this story. 'My footprints are probably there as well. I hope no one comes checking,' she said, worried.

'Shepard's not going to set the police on a twelve-year-old girl . . . probably,' said Jake. He thought for a moment. 'Actually, maybe you should chuck the shoes away.'

'I can't. My dad'll notice.' She looked ruefully at her incriminating feet.

'Have we got any sandpaper?' asked Ben.

'Mmm, I think so,' said Jake. Ben looked at him patiently. 'Oh, I see,' he added, and wandered off to find it.

'Here you go.' He handed it to Ben, who picked up Millie's feet one by one and sanded the base of each shoe in a few small places.

'What are you doing?' Jake asked. 'Those are Millie's shoes you're wrecking, you little monster.'

'I'm not wrecking them. It's just that if anyone did check, they'd have a different wear pattern from the prints they've got from the lab.'

Jake grinned. 'Smartarse.'

'Mum says you're not supposed to call me that.'

'If Mum was here, she'd call you that, too.'

By lunchtime, Edward Davies was outside the lab again, reporting that the staff had all left and the building seemed to have been shut up. Only the security man who had pulled faces at Millie still appeared to be working there. Another journalist was at Playmatic's head office in Milton Keynes.

'It looks evil, that building,' sniffed Max.

Playmatic still refused to comment on camera, but they had issued a statement which the man read out on air, saying they would never condone or practise any kind of animal testing.

'Yeah, right,' said Ben.

A third reporter was outside Arthur Shepard's home, trying to get an interview from him, but he wasn't there so they couldn't get any comment.

Ben wasn't surprised by this – he had spent some time trying to track Arthur Shepard down with no success. He had no mobile phone registered to him, or to his wife and children, that Ben could discover. He had tried every one of his usual tricks, and some unusual ones too, but to no avail. He kept apologising to Max for being so unhelpful – they all knew every day that went past would surely make it harder to find Celeste, and less likely that they would be able to rescue her. But none of them had any more ideas of where she might be. All they did have was the hope that with so much public attention on him, he probably wouldn't be moving Celeste anywhere or stealing any more cats, because he would surely be recognised.

They munched their way through every snack Jake and Ben's parents had in the house as they watched more of the story on TV. A woman interviewed the journalist who'd taken the pictures at the lab before it was shut down. He claimed that he had seen cat hairs all over the top corridor, and that he had removed some for testing. They had identified hair from at least eleven cats. The news programme then showed the photo of Max that Ben had taken, saying there was little doubt this had come from inside the laboratory.

'This is perfect,' gloated Ben.

'I think I could have done a better face,' moaned Max.

Later that day, Vakkson issued a statement saying that Arthur Shepard hadn't worked for them for some time and had rented the building for a private project. The cameras outside Playmatic were now trained on several hundred protesters, who were accusing the company of being thieves, torturers and murderers. Playmatic issued another statement saying that this was all a mistake and that they had never worked with Arthur Shepard. The tabloids went crazy and printed copies of the emails Ben had tricked from Arthur Shepard, and the picture of Max. Playmatic called them fakes, but no one believed them. A journalist asked them what their secret

Christmas toy was, if not anything to do with these missing cats. They produced a feeble-looking Frisbee substitute that fooled no one.

Scott Bradley's newspaper was now running a competition – if your cat had gone missing and had recently reappeared, it was worth asking it a few questions to see if it could talk, because they were offering forty thousand pounds for an exclusive interview with one of the kidnapped cats.

'Forty thousand pounds,' said Jake hungrily, eyeing Max.

'Not a chance,' said the cat calmly. 'They have all the evidence they need. What kind of publicity-hungry idiot would put himself up for public inspection?'

Chapter Forty

That evening, Millie had left her dad downstairs after dinner, hoping he didn't think she was avoiding him. Max was lying casually on her chair, and she was sitting reading a book, something she felt she hadn't done in weeks. She was surprised by the phone ringing.

'Turn on your TV right now,' said Ben, and promptly hung up.

Millie flicked on the television. Max had opened one eye when the phone rang, a trick Millie longed to be able to do herself. They both watched as the screen came to life, hearing a familiar voice before they saw the matching face.

'Obviously, it's been a very difficult time . . .' Millie looked at Max in horror, but it was true. There was Ariston, being interviewed by Patricia Forsyth on the news programme. 'Yes, of course, I do feel my feline rights have been violated,' he was saying.

'Oh no,' whispered Millie. 'What if he tells them about us

breaking in? We could go to prison. Well, *I* could. Well, a young offenders' institution. You'd probably be sent to a home for criminal cats.'

'Shh,' said the cat, who was still watching the screen intently. 'I think you are safe.'

'How did you escape?' asked the breathless reporter, her face an image of sympathy and admiration.

'There are some things which must remain secret,' said Ariston, sounding more pompous than ever. 'But, suffice it to say that we would all still be in the laboratory if it hadn't been for my bravery and cunning.'

'The cheek!' said Millie.

'I knew he couldn't pass up the chance to say he was the hero,' said Max. 'You'll be fine, Millie. None of the other cats will talk, I don't think. None of them would want this.' He jerked his head at the television, where Ariston's PR agent was explaining that his client had no more time for this interview, as he had to be at a photo shoot in ten minutes.

Arthur Shepard's house was now being watched by about twenty television crews. Eventually, his wife appeared on the doorstep and told them that he no longer lived with her and their children, so could the media please leave them alone. She had no idea where he was nor, she hastily pointed out, did she especially care. This was apparently connected with the fact that another tabloid had printed a story from one of the

Haverham employees saying that they had had no idea what was happening on the third floor, but that Shepard was having an affair with his secretary.

'He didn't seem the type to have an affair with anyone,' said Millie, pulling a disgusted face. 'I mean, urgh.'

'Not urgh,' said Max urgently. '*Aha.*'

'Aha?' She was puzzled for a moment, then her face cracked into a smile. 'Oh, yes. Aha.'

Chapter Forty-One

And so the next morning Millie and Max went back to see Jake and Ben. Finally, they had an idea who might be holding Celeste.

'It's his secretary,' said Millie, as she almost tripped into their hall.

'Is it?' asked Jake, alarmed. 'Where?' He looked out into the street, expecting to see a woman with a notepad and pencil hoving into view.

'We think that's where he's got Celeste,' said Max. 'At his secretary's house. They were having an affair.'

'Really?' said Ben, who'd come to find out what all the noise was about. 'Urgh.'

'I know – but it helps us, doesn't it?' said Millie. 'I mean, we don't think Celeste is at Shepard's place. We know she wasn't kept in the lab, because that journalist went in and poked around, and he would have seen her. We know she wasn't at the houses of his security men, because Max went and looked and couldn't find any sign of her.'

'Celeste was not there,' Max agreed.

'I reckon they've gone away,' added Jake. 'I've been past their places a couple more times, and I haven't seen anybody around, or even a car on the driveway.'

'So, surely it's possible that Celeste is with this woman,' said Millie. 'It's the best lead we have.'

None of them said it, but they were all thinking that it was, in fact, the *only* lead they had, so they had better hope it was good.

'Do we know her surname?' asked Jake, as they trooped upstairs.

'No,' Millie said. 'She just introduced herself as Elaine to me, and they called her his secretary on the news. Someone must have got her full name by now, though.'

They waited patiently as Ben typed various combinations of words into a range of search engines.

'No good,' he said, annoyed.

'Hold on,' said Jake, and disappeared. He returned ten minutes later with a pile of that morning's tabloids. 'These guys make you look like an amateur, mate,' he said, dropping the papers on the desk.

They all began to pore through the articles, which were indeed full of extraordinary details, until Ben shouted triumphantly. 'Elaine *Peters*,' he said. 'Now' – he turned back to his computer – 'where are you hiding, lady?'

Two minutes later, they were looking at her address. 'Hold

on,' said Ben. 'I'll get us an aerial photo.' He typed a few more words. 'There,' he said. 'Ooh, she's got a garden shed.'

'What better place to imprison a cat?' asked Max.

'Exactly,' said Ben. 'Shall we go and get her?'

'Hold on, hold on,' said Jake. 'No one's going anywhere until we've got a proper plan.'

Ben wrinkled his nose in disappointment and Max hissed.

'He's right,' said Millie, reaching over to Max and stroking his back gently. 'We can't just wander up to her front door, ask ourselves in, sneak into the garden and steal back Celeste – always presuming that's where she is,' she added, trying her hardest not to tempt fate.

'We could threaten her,' Ben suggested cheerily, eyeing his water pistol again.

'No,' said Jake firmly. 'No one is going to be threatened with guns, even ones that just squirt water. We could be arrested. We'll have to be a bit more discreet. And a lot more legal.'

'Could we get over the fence to the back garden?' asked Millie, scanning the aerial photo.

'I think so,' said Ben, looking regretfully once more at the water pistol. It was hardly worth having it at all. 'She could see us, though, from the back windows.'

'Hmm.' Millie thought for a moment. 'Not if we provide some sort of distraction at the front of the house. Who has the most innocent face?'

'You,' said Jake simply.

'It can't be Millie,' Max pointed out. 'They've met, remember? She knows what Millie looks like.'

'Fair point,' said Jake. 'Then it's Ben. That's not saying much, by the way.'

'OK,' said Millie. 'Ben provides the diversion, Jake and I steal Celeste. Max keeps a lookout. Agreed?'

'I hate being the diversion.' Ben looked sulky. 'Why do I have to be a diversion?'

'Jake was the diversion last time,' said Millie soothingly. 'You probably won't even get chased by dogs.'

Ben looked even more disappointed at the prospect of not being chased by dogs, but there was really no alternative.

'And we'll need your bike,' said Millie to Jake.

'Er, OK,' he said. 'You remember it's broken?'

'Exactly,' she said, and smiled.

Chapter Forty-Two

'It's too big for him,' said Jake critically, as they wheeled the injured bike through the streets. Max was once again hiding in Millie's bag, to avoid attracting attention as they walked along together.

'I know,' she admitted. 'I don't think Elaine Peters will notice, though. She didn't strike me as much of a cycling expert.'

'How long were you with her for?' asked Ben, curious.

'In total?' she said. 'About four minutes, I think.'

'Oh, right,' said Jake. 'Well, you probably know her as well as anyone, then.'

Millie pulled a face. She knew it was a bit of a risk, but Jake wasn't so much taller than Ben, and the bike was unrideable anyway. They were almost at Elaine Peters's road, and it was time for them to separate.

'Are you sure you know what you've got to do?' asked Jake.

Ben nodded.

'Max?' said Millie.

The cat jumped out of her bag and nodded too. 'I'll be at the front of the house,' he said. 'If I see any sign of Arthur Shepard, I'll yowl like this.' He gave a blood-curdling cry.

'Yes, that'll do it,' said Jake, jumping visibly. 'It would certainly get my attention.'

'And if anything happens to you,' said Millie to Ben, 'you have my alarm?' She had a personal attack alarm that Bill's overly cautious wife had given her when she got her first bicycle, 'just in case', as she had rather unnervingly put it. At the time Millie had thought, rather ungraciously, that a set of lights would have been a more suitable present, but the alarm, which could be heard up to a half-mile away, was something she was now delighted to give to Ben to make sure he could alert them if anything went wrong.

'And we meet back here in fifteen minutes?' asked Jake.

'Yes,' they replied as one, and looked nervously at each other.

'Let's go,' said Millie.

She and Jake disappeared down a narrow lane which would take them to the fields at the back of Elaine Peters's house.

Ben and Max, following at a discreet distance, and mostly under hedgerow, went the opposite way. Max settled himself under a large shrub a few houses up from their target. Ben looked around to make sure there were no passers-by watching, although this was a small, residential street, and heaved his rather short legs onto the bike. He hoped that no one was looking out of a window to notice that his feet didn't come near to reaching the pedals and that his bike was crumpled beyond repair.

He waited patiently for a car to drive past, hoping that it would be soon – he was getting anxious. Although he had longed to be part of the rescue mission last time, he had known that sitting at home, hacking into computer systems, was his real strength. He wasn't sure he had the necessary skills for what he was about to do. A few seconds later he was rewarded as a delivery van from a supermarket swept past him at high speed. The road was narrow and Ben hurled himself into it as the van sped off, shrieking loudly.

'Ow! Ow!' he hollered. 'Owww.' Nothing happened. He waited, and shouted again. 'Owwwww.'

Elaine Peters's door opened a crack.

'Oh!' she cried, and ran out into the street. 'Don't move! Are you hurt?'

'Yes,' said Ben – not quite lying, as he had obtained some good grazes when he fell onto the gravelly road.

'Oh dear. Let me call an ambulance,' she said.

'No, no,' said Ben hurriedly, realising that he would be exposed as a fraud in five seconds flat if medical professionals were involved. 'He . . . er,' Ben cast around for something to say. He wished he'd practised this instead of the stupid piano.

'He didn't hit me quite, just clipped my wheel, and I fell. Nothing's broken. I mean, except my bike.'

'Let me ring your mother, then. What's her number?' said Elaine Peters.

'My mother's dead. Car accident,' Ben improvised.

'Oh, no! Your father, then?'

'He's away,' said Ben. 'At sea.'

Two houses away, a shrub started giggling.

'Away at sea?' asked Elaine Peters, appalled. 'Who's looking after you?'

'My brother,' said Ben. 'But he's in, er, London today. He'll be home later. I don't want to bother him. He'll be angry with me for breaking my bike.'

'Well, perhaps I could take you home,' she said doubtfully, looking back at her front door.

'No, really,' said Ben. 'You've been very kind already. I only live a few streets away – I can walk home. I'll be able to get up in just a minute.'

He crawled feebly towards the kerb and she bent down to help him.

Chapter Forty-Three

Millie and Jake heard Ben's shouts from the other side of the house. They were already in place behind the fence and peered quickly through its slats to check the whereabouts of the shed – which looked gratifyingly old, and not at all a state-of-the-art secure facility. This was their cue. Jake gave Millie a boost over the fence, then leapt over himself. They both had their hoods up, just in case the neighbours were looking out of their back windows, instead of being safely at work as Millie was hoping. They ran to the shed and tapped softly on the door.

'Celeste?' whispered Millie, feeling both nervous that the cat wouldn't be inside and a little stupid talking to a wooden door. 'Celeste? Are you in there? It's Millie.'

''Allo?' said an unmistakably French cat.

The door was locked and Jake stood back. 'Careful,' he said. He thumped it hard. The damp wood around the lock splintered and cracked. 'And again,' he muttered, and hit it a second time.

The door swung open and the eyes of a beautiful tortoiseshell cat met theirs as Millie opened a cage door to free her for a second time.

'*Déjà vu*, hmm?' asked Celeste.

'I know,' said Millie. 'We came as soon as we realised where you were.'

'Thank you,' she said. 'Is Max here?'

'He's keeping watch at the front,' Millie replied, as they ran back to the fence. Celeste squeezed under it as Millie and Jake hefted themselves over it once again. 'Let's go.'

They ran back to the agreed meeting place, where Ben, limping slightly, and Max were waiting for them.

'Celeste!' cried Max. 'We have found you.' He ran up to her and they rubbed cheeks, their whiskers entangled.

'Second time lucky, as I think you say over here,' she said, looking at Millie, who nodded, not wanting to correct her.

'Thank you,' said Celeste. 'You are a hero, Max.' She gazed at him. '*My* hero,' she breathed.

'Is he blushing?' Ben whispered loudly.

Max made a dignified swish of his tail. 'Celeste and I have to do some . . .' He looked at her, unsure of the phrase he wanted.

'Catching up?' she suggested.

'Some catching up,' Max continued. 'I shall meet you at home later, Millie. I shall see you two' – he jerked his head at Jake and Ben, who were trying, and failing, to contain their sniggering – 'another day. Perhaps tomorrow.'

'OK,' said Jake.

'Sorry,' added Ben.

They both started to giggle.

'Thank you for helping to rescue Celeste,' Max finished, looking at them all with a stern expression.

'Any time,' said Millie, whose nostrils were now flaring suspiciously.

'*A bientôt*,' said Celeste, as she and Max began to walk away.

'Not if we see them first,' Max muttered.

Chapter Forty-Four

That evening, Celeste had already begun her journey home and Max would say nothing about her, except that she lived very near to Brussels, and that they had arranged to meet again soon. He and Millie were at home, watching the late news. The director of Playmatic had resigned, saying he needed to spend more time with his family. The board had followed. All their families had been pining for them too, it seemed. Arthur Shepard was revealed to be in the Maldives, applying frantically, but unsuccessfully, for new jobs. Elaine Peters's cat burglary did not make even the local papers.

Over the next few days, to Millie's great surprise, none of the cats' owners appeared in the news claiming their cats had been made to talk.

'Why do you think that is?' she asked Max, having puzzled over it for some time.

'I don't think they'll have said anything,' said Max.

'The owners?'

'The cats. I wouldn't have, if it hadn't been an emergency. Cats aren't meant to talk. We don't really like it. Well,' he corrected himself, '*I* quite like it. But only because it's been interesting here with you. If I was just in someone's house, saying, "Where's the cat food? No, I didn't leave that mouse there," it would be pretty boring. Plus, the reward was only for the first cat, I think. And they've probably been watching the television and seeing what's happened to Ariston.' Ariston was now slated to front a show called *When Good Pets Go Bad.* Max had put his head in his paws for some moments when he heard about it.

'I still can't quite believe we did it,' said Millie.

'I know. There's only one more thing left to do.'

'What's that? Oh.' Her face fell. 'Of course. We need to get you home.'

Max and Millie spent several days trying to work out how she could return him to Brussels. She considered inventing a pen pal who urgently needed her to visit (a sudden desire to improve vernacular English, or only three weeks to live, for example), but realised her dad wasn't an idiot. She hinted that they should maybe go on some sort of brief holiday before she went back to school in two weeks. Her dad didn't seem interested. She even thought of waiting till she was back at school and then proposing it as a school trip, before she gloomily accepted that by the time it had been organised, Max's family would probably have given him up for dead.

They began to plan instead for him to try and get home alone, by Eurostar. But Millie didn't want him to have to get around London on his own. She tried suggesting that a day trip to London would be nice, but her dad was buried in papers and muttered that it would have to wait. Anyway, she really wasn't convinced that Max would be able to get through the security there – it would be like an airport, surely. She still thought a ferry would be easier, although she understood his dislike of the water. But then, how would he get to Dover, and then from Calais to Brussels? Max wasn't so worried about the travelling, but he very much wanted her to come with him and meet Stef and Sofie. They gave themselves one more week to come up with something and then they would give in, and Max would go home on his own. Millie looked desolate at the prospect.

'I'll write,' promised Max.

'You don't have thumbs. You're not a big reader.'

'I'll email. I've been practising. I can tap a computer key with my paw, look.' Max illustrated his new-found skills.

'OK, you can email me,' she sniffed. 'But it won't be the same. And I bet your spelling's awful.'

'Something could still happen,' he said sagely.

And something did.

[illegible]

[illegible]

[illegible]

[illegible]

[illegible]

[illegible]

[illegible]

[illegible]

[illegible]

[illegible]

Chapter Forty-Five

The day before Max was due to head off alone, Millie's dad bounded in through the front door.

'Dad,' said Millie, alarmed. 'Are you all right?'

'I'm better than all right,' he said, picking her up and swinging her around.

Millie had begun to accept that she might never be tall enough for this not to happen, unless she moved to a country populated entirely by Snow White's friends.

'Put me down. What is it?'

'I've got a new job.'

'Really? Where?'

'Anywhere I like! The bank manager has just given my freelance business the go-ahead.'

'Freelance what?'

'Well, I suppose I should have told you before, but you know when I lost my job?'

Millie nodded, astonished. Her dad never mentioned this by choice.

'Well, I didn't lose it because they didn't need me. I lost it because there was a fault in their system, a back door, which they thought I should have noticed – it left them open to hackers.'

'You would never have made that kind of mistake,' Millie snapped.

Her dad beamed at her. 'No,' he continued. 'It turns out I didn't. They had someone inside the department who made the back door deliberately. He was passing on information to a rival company.'

'What a creep.' Millie couldn't help wishing she'd met Ben a bit sooner.

'Quite. I spent two weeks after they kicked me out trying to work out what had happened, and I realised that was the only answer. But it was difficult to convince them that it wasn't just me trying to protect my reputation.'

'Oh! Is *that* what you were doing?' Millie asked, feeling a light bulb come on over her head again. This really had been an educational summer.

'Yes, of course it was.' He looked surprised. 'Why? What did you think I was doing?'

'Dunno. I thought you'd gone a bit mental.'

'Cheek.' Her dad pretended to clip her round the ear as she leaped out of reach and stuck out her tongue.

'Very mature,' he said loftily.

'You started it. How did you convince them, then?' she asked.

'I didn't. I sent them all the information and the conclusions I'd come to, and they ignored me. Then, a couple of weeks ago, I had a call from my old boss.'

'To say sorry?' Millie was feeling a little guilty herself. How could she not have noticed that her dad had been going through all this? She'd been too busy with her own industrial espionage to pay attention to his, she supposed.

'They never say sorry. But, this guy—'

'The creep?' Millie checked.

'The very same. He had defected to their rivals the day before. They were calling to offer me my old job back.'

'Good. But you said no?' She was confused.

'Not completely. I said I'd work for them on a freelance basis, and they could be the first clients of my new computer consultancy,' he replied with a small smile.

'Dad, you don't *have* a computer consultancy,' she pointed out.

'Correction. I didn't have one. I do now.'

'You turned down your old job so you could start your own company?' Millie was amazed and impressed.

'I know.'

He was now almost jigging from one foot to the other, unable to contain his excitement. Millie suppressed a laugh when she realised how much he reminded her of Ben when he had begun persecuting Alan Shepard.

'I thought it was a bit of a risk,' he carried on happily. 'But I want a boss I can trust – me. So, I started to put together a business plan for my own company, arranged a meeting with the bank manager to talk about setting up a business account, and then, of course, everything went crazy.'

'What did?' Millie asked.

'Well, you know how much publicity there's been this month about companies and computer leaks? You know, that case with Vakkson, and Playmatic, and that lab we were cleaning for a few weeks, with Bill? Confidential emails appearing in journalists' in-boxes, and that kind of thing?'

'Mmm?' said Millie casually, looking profoundly shifty. Luckily, her dad was too involved in what he was saying to notice.

'Well, I thought it was the perfect time to send out some stuff to the companies in the area, assuming they're all a bit nervous about their systems being hacked into and read, offering them my amazing computer expertise at a surprisingly affordable price. That's what I've been doing the past couple of weeks. And loads of them are interested – I've had a pile of letters and emails. So I contacted the bank and showed them all the work I could get, and they thought it was a great idea, and now I'm Alan Raven, Freelance Computer Engineer and Troubleshooter.'

'That's so cool. I'm really proud of you, Dad.'

'Thanks, love.' He gave her a quick hug, and added, 'I'm going to start next week, just before you go back to school.'

Millie's brain began to tick – if her dad started work before she went back to school, maybe she could sneak down to London, or Dover, and at least get Max part of the way home.

Her dad continued: 'So, how about we go away somewhere for a couple of days, to celebrate?'

'OK, like where?'

'Where would you like to go? Don't say the Bahamas, I haven't earned anything yet.'

Millie couldn't believe her luck.

'Could we, erm, could we go to Brussels? Just for a day or two?'

'Brussels? Why Brussels?'

'I dunno. It sounds nice.' Millie wished she'd asked Max more about his home town, so she could say something a bit more convincing than that. 'The Atomium,' she said, suddenly remembering the huge sculpture that Max had shown her on the net. 'And, uh, the botanical gardens.' So, so feeble. Luckily her dad was distracted.

'Well, all right, then,' he said, undeniably surprised. 'Brussels it is. I've never been there, and we can explore together. I'll book a ferry. We'll go, what, day after tomorrow?'

'Yes. That's brilliant. Thanks, Dad.'

'I'm going to ring Bill and tell him the news. He'll need some new assistants, if we're not around.'

'OK.' Millie disappeared upstairs and shut her door. Max flew out from under the bed. 'Did you hear all that?'

He nodded, and raced round her legs like a demented kitten. Then he remembered the ferry and sobered up. Not that he minded the water so much this time. He was going home.

Chapter Forty-Six

Two days later, Max stowed safely inside her bag, Millie and her dad breezed through customs, who happily cared far more about cats coming *into* the country than going out, and not very much about those. Max didn't enjoy the Channel any more the second time than he had the first, but at least this would be the last trip across it he had to make. Millie's dad drove them to Brussels and they checked into their hotel. It was mid-afternoon.

'Where do you want to go first?' asked her dad.

This time, Millie was ready. Max had prepared her with information about useful tourist sites near his home.

'Can we go to the Horta Museum?'

'Sure. What is it?'

'Horta was an Art Nouveau architect. It's supposed to be great.' She brandished a guidebook at him. 'It's on Rue Américaine. That's not too far to walk.' And it was two minutes from Max's house.

‘I didn’t know you were interested in Art Nouveau,’ said her dad, as they began to walk up the vast Avenue Louise.

‘Well, I’m a very mysterious child,’ she said.

‘You really are,’ he said, squeezing her shoulder as they went.

Ten minutes and only one wrong turning later (helpfully signalled by Max shoving a paw into Millie’s ribs), they were on his road. The plan was to stop at the Église Sainte-Trinité, a church right by Max’s house, wander in with her dad, wait till he was looking at something, and then sneak outside and say goodbye to Max. Millie was simultaneously excited that the plan was in action and distraught that she would soon lose Max. But she couldn’t let her dad see any of this. She tried not to think about it at all, but, inevitably, all she could think about then was not thinking about Max. She thought about how much she missed her friends when they just went on holiday for a few weeks, and could barely stop herself from crying at the thought of losing her best friend for ever.

They had spent their last day together yesterday, and had gone to say goodbye to Jake and Ben. Max had promised to keep in touch with them, too.

It seemed only moments ago that they had said goodbye to the boys, and now they were down to their last few minutes together.

‘Let’s go in here, Dad,’ she said. ‘It’s baroque.’ She had no idea what that meant, but it was, according to the guide, a useful fact about the church, and she had to get her dad inside.

He looked puzzled, but wandered in and began to look around the interior. Millie slipped back outside, opened her bag, and let Max out.

'Here you go,' she whispered. 'Home.'

'Thank you,' he said, as she hugged him. 'We'll meet again, Millie, I promise. And soon.'

She nodded, knowing that if she said anything, she'd cry, and that that would be even harder to hide from her dad.

'I have to go.'

'You've got my address. And the phone number,' Max checked, but he knew she had written them down carefully the night before. 'And my email.' Millie had set him up an account, too. 'And I have yours.' He had committed them firmly to memory.

Millie kissed the top of his head, ruffled his fur, and put him down.

'*A bientôt*,' he said.

'See you soon,' she replied, blinking hard.

She hurried back indoors and, before her eyes could adapt to the darkness, straight into the arms of her father. He looked at her carefully.

'Why don't you see him home?' he said. 'Say goodbye properly.'

Millie looked at him in astonishment. If her dad became any more unexpected, she might have to start paying more attention to him.

'Dad?'

'Go on, before you miss him. I'll come along in a few minutes, check his family aren't too weird. Well, no weirder than ours, anyway.'

Millie reached up and hugged him. And then she ran out of the church.

'Max!' she shouted. 'Max!'

'Shhh,' hissed the cat, reappearing beside her like a shadow. 'Your dad will hear. What is it?'

'Max, isn't it?' said her dad, walking out behind them.

It was the first and last time in their acquaintance that Millie saw the cat entirely lost for words.

'Yes,' she said, for him. 'This is Max. Max, this is my dad. Turns out we're not the only ones keeping secrets.'

'You do seem to have got my daughter into some awful habits,' said Millie's dad mildly.

'Er,' said Max. 'Hello. Yes, sorry about that. It was just burglary, really.'

'Hush,' said her dad, smiling. 'I don't want to hear any more. I'll only worry.'

'How long have you known?' asked the cat rather weakly.

'Saw your eyes under Millie's bed. That was the first night in our house, wasn't it?' he answered. 'And then a couple of days later, that woman at the lab asked me and Bill if we'd seen a missing cat. I don't really believe in coincidences.'

'Why didn't you mention it?' asked Millie.

'You needed a summer project,' her dad said. 'And I thought this would be more interesting than cleaning windows, so I left you to it. I figured you'd call me if you needed help, or you got out of your depth.'

Millie and Max looked at each other, thinking it was probably best if he never knew the details.

He looked directly at Max. 'I didn't know for sure that you were one of the talking ones, like that marmalade-coloured nightmare on the news, but it seemed a good bet. And I know my daughter well enough to assume you wouldn't be a nightmare. Now,' he continued. 'Your family, Max? Can we meet them?'

'Of course,' said Max. 'It will be my pleasure. It's this way.' And he trotted in front of them, not caring at all that people might think it looked odd.

Millie's dad put his arm across her shoulders, and the two of them followed Max up the street.

About the Author

Natalie Haynes has been a stand-up comedian since she graduated in 1996, though she briefly taught Latin and Greek as well. Her first solo show, *Six Degrees of Desolation*, was nominated for the Perrier Best Newcomer Award in 2002 and since then she has completed five national tours, as well as performing in New York, and even Berlin.

Natalie also makes programmes for Radio 4, most recently *Laughing Matters* and *Classical Comedy*. She is a regular guest on *Front Row* and *Loose Ends* and *Newsnight Review*. She is also a guest columnist for the *The Times*. She is vegetarian and lives in London.

'The country's leading young female stand-up – she's shrewd, witty, talented and mightily intelligent' – *Time Out*

www.nataliehaynes.com/thegreatescape

3 8002 01546 7964